TRAVELS WITH RUSI

IN
SOUTHERN INDIA

TRAVELS WITH RUSI

IN
SOUTHERN INDIA

MAC ROGERS

ATHENA PRESS
LONDON

ISBN: 978 1 84748 293 8

First published 2008 by
ATHENA PRESS
Queen's House, 2 Holly Road
Twickenham TW1 4EG
United Kingdom

Printed for Athena Press

For Maggie,
without whose vision
and enthusiasm this book would
not have been possible

FOREWORD

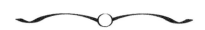

This is a lively, autobiographical and very pleasing travel book. Most of us, unlike this author, cannot spend the time on leisurely, informed and worthwhile travel, but one of the lessons of this charming book is that, with increasing retirement and consequent leisure time available to everyone, we will all probably have the opportunity. A book like this is just the spur that we might need to turn a dream into a reality that we will always remember.

Mac Rogers celebrates the joy of travel, the get-up-and-go spirit and this is a book that will be great for the traveller – even of the armchair variety – who wants to share his experience.

The next thing about this book is that it will encourage other people to do just the same thing; to rattle round the world when they might be pruning the roses in Bexhill (not that there is anything the matter with that!) and from this experience to gain something of value that will stay with them all their lives.

Mark Sykes

tuesday, 23 january 2001

Would it live up to our expectations? We had done it before. The second time better than the first. A third time was surely risky. Too late to ponder that now, we were there – outside Bangalore Airport – where we had had to wait for an age for our cases to revolve. I was beginning to believe we would never see them again, when hey, presto, before you could say '*Sai Ram*', they appeared – as if by magic.

Would Rusi be there? This was our next concern. Maggie felt he might be but I doubted it. As head of the firm, he would be in bed at 3.30 a.m. in preparation for an arduous drive ahead.

We looked anxiously at the waiting crowds behaving as if it were midday. No Rusi, but there instead was Peter, who held up a board inscribed 'Mac and Maggie'.

He greeted us with a hugely warm smile when we made ourselves known. He had waited for over an hour. Swiftly, he took us to a new hotel – the Samraz – where we dreamily signed in and staggered into bed.

I failed to find the light switch and was about to get into bed with the lights blazing when I realised that the lights worked on a key system, and that the removal of the key from a wall bracket achieved the desired darkness.

We had told Peter to inform Rusi that we would be up at about 11.30 a.m. and ready to start the day's adventures.

Consequently we were a little surprised to be awoken by the bedside telephone at 9.30 a.m. Rusi had come some two hours early. He was just the same and wanted to know if we wanted to start our journey today or tomorrow.

'Today!' we chorused spontaneously. 'Today, Rusi. Today we want!'

'OK,' he said. 'I'll send Peter for you at twelve noon.'

Our third journey in Southern India and our travels with Rusi were about to begin.

Amid growing feelings of excitement, Maggie and I went up a floor to the roof garden and had a lovely breakfast – dosas, scrambled eggs, and a pot of coffee.

Peter arrived and drove us to Whitefield, a prosperous suburb of Bangalore. En route, Peter pointed out Sai Baba's wonderful new hospital, which took under a year to build and was opened by the Prime Minister only last Friday. Apparently, queues of people gathered every day for free treatment.

Peter confided that he never went to school. He couldn't read or write but had a very clever wife. He told us that Rusi was his guru and that he taught him to drive.

Rusi's new house – 'The Garden of Allah' – was lovely. Zarrine, Rusi's sister, and Viraf, her husband, lived opposite. Almost immediately, Maggie went to Zarrine with a present of chocolates, but not before we inspected the orchard. Wonderful! Maggie, with characteristic generosity, gave Dinu, Rusi's wife, lovely chocolates, soap, lipsticks and a candle.

While we enjoyed a delicious meal of chicken curry, rice and vegetable curry, Rusi went out and purchased two cases of water (sealed, of course – this is India!), bananas and oranges. At 3 p.m. sharp, we set off!

Before we left Bangalore I went to Thomas Cook and changed my Marks and Spencer traveller's cheques into rupees.

The drive was wonderful – so rural, so truly rural. We saw heaps of egrets – birds we search for in Europe. We stopped in a hotel for tea, had our first masala dosa and visited our first (of many) filthy loos. But of course, we consoled ourselves with 'this is India.'

Soon it was the 'dust hour'. Everyone and everything was going home: 'The ploughman homeward plods his weary way.'*

This is what it must have been like in Gray's day, in eighteenth-century England, with weary walkers and waggoners trekking home at the close of day.

> The day thou gavest, Lord, is ended,
> The darkness falls at thy behest.

> From: 'The Day Thou Gavest, Lord is Ended'
> John Ellerton

In India there is continual movement along the roadside. Young children, in pristine clothes, striding out to school; saried women skilfully balancing impossible loads on their beautiful heads moving relentlessly and gracefully to the next village; pilgrims, dressed in green and orange and black, tirelessly seeking their ultimate spiritual goal.

This is how it must have been in England before the advent of the motor car, with wayside travellers whom you never see now.

Ten bullock carts laden with sugar beet passed by on the other side. For them, it was the end of the working day.

Before Mysore we stopped for the night. Rusi found us a lovely hotel in a garden – the first of many we hoped. The room was good but the loo wasn't clean and Maggie sent for the manager, who cleaned it himself.

We had a good supper but we were all very tired. Rusi was as lovely as ever. 'Saint Rusi' Maggie called him, before we bade him goodnight and quickly fell asleep.

---

* From: Gray, Thomas 'Elegy Written in a Country Churchyard'

Wednesday, 24 January

After a hearty breakfast consisting of very hard toast, a pot of milky coffee and a bowl of soggy cornflakes with hot milk (not a happy combination), we hit the road. Rusi had planned a treat. He had, since our last visit, discovered a bird sanctuary at Shrirangapatnam.

We arrived at 9.30 a.m. to find a haven of peace with a lake and luscious vegetation. The Garden of Eden must have been like this. Such peace! And so many birds – hundreds of them. They remained still as you approached them – not like England, when you have to fumble hurriedly for your binoculars and they fly away after a hasty glimpse! Here they stayed to be admired.

'Why don't they fly away, Rusi, when you approach them?'

'Because they trust you. They have learnt that you are not going to harm them, and consequently, they are not afraid. Aggression provokes fear. Here there is no aggression.'

'Thank you, Rusi, for those words of wisdom. Rusi the philosopher!'

Oh, such peace! Such bliss! To get away from the hordes, the traffic and the tensions.

Rusi hired a boat and we all clambered in. Govinder, a tall, swarthy Sikh, rowed us. He was very knowledgeable. He pointed out and identified all the birds. The trees were full of them: grey stone plovers, river terns, peacocks, grey herons, painted storks, night herons, cliff swallows, pied kingfishers, purple herons, marsh herons and there were trees covered in giant bats, hanging upside down.

Once ashore, we were besieged by a bus of schoolchildren asking to take our photographs. Apparently we are a rare species – a white couple!

We drove on to Mysore. The traffic was preposterous, so hectic, and after the tranquillity of the bird sanctuary it seemed really crazy. Rusi showed us the beautiful palace, but we didn't get out as we saw it before, five years ago, on our very first trip. Been there, done that! How blasé can you get?

The roads were all abustle with vehicles of all kinds – Ambassadors, rickshaws, lorries and cycles – pushing for position, horns blaring! Perpetual motion; perpetual noise till at long last we left the towns behind and found ourselves on a country drive through villages. They were very primitive. Maggie needed a bathroom stop, as Rusi so delicately put it, and she went behind a bush. So much cleaner, she said, and added, 'It's all so rural and agricultural round here.'

She wasn't feeling too good and was obviously in need of sustenance. Since the onset of diabetes the previous year she had found she must eat and drink at regular intervals, otherwise her energy level declined.

It was now 2 p.m. and we'd had no lunch, but suddenly Rusi pulled up and parked beside a roadside hut, which was very clean with good hand-washing facilities. After puris and a milky coffee, Maggie felt better. The puris were good, although fried.

On to Bandipur National Park. What an amazing drive! We went through terrain containing monkeys, wild boar and mynah birds, which are so pretty in flight. This is the area they call 'the jungle'.

At a rural checkpoint the police stopped us and asked if we had any liquor in the boot. Rusi was very firm with them and they abandoned the intended search. But where would we be without him? Rusi was convinced they would have taken money from us, as the police are very corrupt.

Time to find accommodation, so we consulted the book. Tiger Trails, described as a lodge, was favourite, but we failed to find it and instead we chanced upon Bamboo Banks Farm, where there was one dreamlike cottage free. Built in stone, it stood aloof in a clearing of the forest. It had a marvellous shower. Rusi stayed inside with us in an adjoining children's room. Maggie was much relieved, as the cottage was quite isolated and the animals roamed at night. With the protection of an electric fence and Rusi's reassuring presence, we reckoned we'd be all right, though what he'd do if a tiger called I didn't know.

Dinner was served alfresco at 8 p.m. We could hardly believe our eyes – the places were laid on a marble table with silver candlesticks and cotton napkins.

The other guests, all Indian, were relatives, and they occupied the three remaining cottages. One couple came from Goa, one couple came from Mumbai, another couple from Mill Hill in England and a single elderly man from Guildford.

They went indoors to the bar while we sat at the long marble table so impressively decked out. Once more we had fallen on our feet, and commenced the meal in an extremely happy frame of mind. It was 'a beauteous evening, calm and free'* and the food was superb for £4 a head. We could hardly believe our luck... until the owner joined us. He, like Rusi, was a Parsee and that's all they had in common. He was the most politically incorrect person Maggie and I had ever met. He was a powerful landowning tea planter with massive estates – a dinosaur from the days of the Raj. He was completely fascist in all his views, which he

---

* From: Wordsworth, William, *Miscellaneous Sonnets*, Part One, Section xxx

expressed all the time. He monopolised the conversation. He had done everything. He mourned the loss of the tiger shoots and detested the eco-warriors, who 'simply meddle', while 'all social workers pussyfoot around'. Maggie winced and bravely took issue, but to no avail. He didn't listen to a word she said. He arrogantly dismissed the legal system as inappropriate, and considered that all criminals should be hanged or shot.

Meanwhile we enjoyed a magnificent meal: consommé soup and garlic bread with home-made scones for starters, followed by a liberal and diverse buffet.

We bade goodnight to mine host, who appeared impervious to our rising anger. He had been impossible and insufferable, using his position as host to propound his totally unacceptable views.

thursday, 25 january

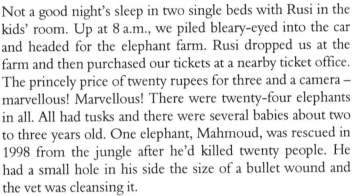

Not a good night's sleep in two single beds with Rusi in the kids' room. Up at 8 a.m., we piled bleary-eyed into the car and headed for the elephant farm. Rusi dropped us at the farm and then purchased our tickets at a nearby ticket office. The princely price of twenty rupees for three and a camera – marvellous! Marvellous! There were twenty-four elephants in all. All had tusks and there were several babies about two to three years old. One elephant, Mahmoud, was rescued in 1998 from the jungle after he'd killed twenty people. He had a small hole in his side the size of a bullet wound and the vet was cleansing it.

Suddenly masses of monkeys arrived, sensing that food was at hand and eager to eat all the scraps.

The elephant boys prepared all the food which looked like balls of dough with white on the outside. Each boy was responsible for feeding his own elephant. Some big elephants got four balls, the size of mini footballs. Afterwards, coconuts were put into their mouths and we saw their huge tongues and teeth. Not a pretty sight!

We stayed there for one-and-a-half hours, fascinated. While the elephants ate and the monkeys frolicked about on the grass making occasional hazardous sorties into the elephants' compound.

Rusi fetched the car and we drove back along country lanes naturally festooned with flowers, predominantly pink, as we turned into the drive of Bamboo Banks. What a journey! It beggared all description like Cleopatra's barge.

Breakfast was delicious in the same idyllic setting. The cook was sweet so Maggie said, and we had pineapple juice, papaya, super toast made on a spit, plus delectable dosas and omelettes – something for everybody's taste.

Mine host came and sat with us again – and argued – but we tactfully avoided confrontation. We couldn't be bothered to challenge his fascist nonsense.

Stuffed, we wandered back to our dream cottage, firstly through a garden of colourful odoriferous flowers and then a wild walk through pink blossom trees covered in blue convolvulus. We packed quickly and the houseman came for our bags. I paid a bill of £54, which covered everything – accommodation, dinner and breakfast for three! Rusi's bedroom cost only 200 rupees!

We said fond farewells to the large Indian party and our host and hostess, Mr and Mrs Kothavalla.

We had seen very little of her, but I am sure she was responsible for the cultural ambience which pervades this idyllic spot. It's a veritable paradise, where they have lived for twenty-seven years. Maggie loved it and vowed to return, if only to savour the tea which is grown on the estate.

'Y'know those hurricane lamps which were hanging on branches in our bedroom?' said Maggie.

'Mmh?' I replied.

'Well, we could hang our lamps in the cottage in Gelliwen like that. All we need to do is select appropriate branches and attach them to a simple piece of wood which you can screw into the wall. OK?'

'Mmh,' I replied, pensively.

On the road once more we had the most amazing journey over the rolling hills. There were thirty-six hairpin bends in all as we went onwards and upwards. Rusi drove brilliantly, avoiding potholes and maniac drivers. We were safe, but there were many near misses on the bends. The hills went on for miles and miles. There were heaps of eucalyptus trees and 'Jesus Loves You' painted neatly on the rocks.

Finally, we arrived at Hilltop Ooty and, at 2.30 p.m., Rusi found the government hotel where we last stayed on New Year's Eve in 1995 – Hotel Mayura. Rusi went in and booked two rooms, obtaining a discount: 650 rupees each.

As we were exhausted by the mountain drive we slept for a couple of hours in our newly acquired Room 101, which I vaguely remembered had sinister implications in Orwell's *1984*. It was a vast room with a fireplace and must, in its day, have been magnificent. Now it was ill-furnished and dilapidated, run down. I felt that oak panelling would help restore its former beauty.

Rusi joined us in our room for whisky and cheese biscuits and then we all went in to dinner. There were no other guests... Ominous! The meal was truly awful. Rice, vegetable curry and Manchurian vegetables, served by a coughing, spluttering old man in a woollen hat. He had a huge aquiline nose which threatened to drip into the dal at any moment.

Having got that over, we returned to bed and read. I slept fitfully but Maggie didn't wake till morning. She sleeps so much better in India.

friday, 26 january

Up at 9.30 a.m. and off to Hotel Lake View for breakfast. We couldn't face the sniffing waiter. We found that the hotel was good and reasonably priced. Rusi discovered that we could move into a cottage for 650 rupees. However, we didn't feel like moving. The breakfast was splendid and I began to perk up: cornflakes, toast, plain dosas and lovely coffee for only £2.

In spite of the name, the view of the lake from the hotel was disappointing, so we decided to take a closer look and we had a marvellous lakeside drive. There was a ghastly weed covering half of the lake which Rusi said was costly to remove and no one was prepared to foot the bill, so the wretched weed flourished, creeping on and on, unchecked. Ever on the lookout for birds, we were delighted to see three painted storks in a wayside aviary, caged in a vast green net. We felt sorry for them. They had none of the freedom which we experienced in the Mysore Sanctuary. 'We think caged birds sing, when indeed they cry.'*

Ooty, the town, is magic. We had little time to explore it the last time we went. It is a town of many contrasts. It has a very busy bus station, many market stalls, multitudes of Indian people and not a Brit in sight.

We got to the Botanical Gardens, unimpressive on a cold misty morning in 1995, but now bursting with activity and thriving in the sun. Outside the gardens,

---

* Webster, John *The White Devil*, IV.4.124

Maggie purchased a straw hat for twenty rupees (a bargain by anyone's standards). We perambulated peacefully along the garden path. It was too early in the year for a profusion of flowers, but there was a beautiful box hedge, like the one the children love in Gelliwen, as well as lilac and rhododendron trees. It would be lovely there in the spring and summer.

Once outside we visited a herbal shop. There was an anti-diabetes drink for £4 and Maggie was tempted, but Rusi moved us on, wanting to try another shop, saying we would return. Of course we never did. She who hesitates, loses the antidote.

Rusi's chemist was more upmarket, and Maggie settled for two jars of anti-diabetes powder and eucalyptus oil.

The square was full of beggars. It was difficult to make one's way, and I wasn't feeling too well. Maggie thought it might be flu or even the common cold, but I, with typical hypochondria, was convinced that I'd contracted a mild form of malaria!

We decided it was time to have a snack, so we crossed the frantically busy road and visited the Irani Hotel, owned by an Iranian family. The patron was a kindly man but he didn't know Lobat or Shiva, our Persian friends in England. That was reasonable, I suppose, though Lobat was the national poet during the Shah's regime, so it wasn't quite the same as asking someone from South Wales if they knew Dai Jones from Pontypool! We sat at a round table and viewed the street through a plate-glass window. On Rusi's advice we sampled egg parotta (delicious, like an omelette), and drank a pot of tea. Very good value for £2. On the way back our efforts to enter a pretty church (St Stephen's) were thwarted when we found that the gates were locked.

By 3 p.m. we were back again at our government hotel. I withdrew quietly to bed, still feeling under the weather, while Maggie wrote a twelve-page letter to the kids. It was brilliant – so graphic! 'The spontaneous overflow of powerful feelings.'[†]

I woke two hours later and joined my wife outside, who had been continually hailed by passing schoolgirls on their way home from school. 'Hello, Auntie! Where do you come from? What is your name?'

We dressed from six to seven, and Rusi arrived bang on time at the appointed hour for a glass of malt whisky (purchased in the duty-free shop at Heathrow) peanuts and cheesy biscuits. Then off to the Lake View Hotel for supper. Super tomato soup with croutons and cream, and another course to follow: chicken masala for Maggie, paneer in sauce for Rusi, and I had my first ever chicken sizzler. Delicious! And all for £2 a head. The head waiter was charming and so were the rest of his staff, in marked contrast to an arrogant Sikh who was seated at the next table with his very pretty wife. He complained loudly about everything. He should have been staying at our hotel!

Back to our hotel and Room 101. We both agreed that it was really horrid and both slept very badly. Maggie dreamt of her mother and a former boyfriend, as well as an un-known Indian woman screaming in childbirth. It was the worst nightmare she had ever experienced. Meanwhile I dreamt I had Alzheimer's and could not recognise our children. We both awoke feeling distressed. The eerie silence was broken by the sound of a chirruping lizard consuming the remains of a banana in our wastepaper basket. We concluded that the room was haunted and cuddled together to dispel the evil vibes.

[†] From: Wordsworth, William *Preface to Lyrical Ballads*

saturday, 27 january

Republic Day – a time of celebration and a national holiday for India. Nevertheless, tea was brought to our room at 7 a.m. What a relief to see Rusi – so bright in yellow – and the car all shiny and smelling of incense. He had done 'the puja' around the car (a Hindu religious ritual at which offerings are made to the gods in order to seek their favour).

Back to Lake View – and to think we only found it because I needed toast to settle my tummy! Super breakfast: omelettes, iddlies, chutney, toast and jam: £2 for three. Again the service was excellent – charming and efficient. We said goodbye to the waiters and I felt sure we would return.

As we left we looked wistfully at one of the cottages, which had marguerites growing outside. I'm sure we would have slept better there! A different road from Ooty took us downhill through beautiful countryside. What a contrast with the winding, potholed route which we took a day before up to the hill fort from Bamboo Banks! The Nigris Hills are magnificent. On and on we went through villages where everyone was celebrating Republic Day. They were dressed up in their finest apparel, listening to bands and waiting for buses. India is constantly alive, vibrant and colourful, but a special air of celebration pervaded the air that day.

The traffic had been heavy all morning and I felt it was time Rusi took a break. I suggested we have a pot of tea when the opportunity arose. Immediately, as if by magic, a sign to the left appeared, advertising a wayside restaurant in the woods. Ideal! I remembered the words of Sai Baba, the guru whom we planned to visit later in the tour: 'There is no such thing as coincidence.'

'Ask and it shall be given unto you,' sayeth the Lord

Matthew 7:7

The restaurant was breathtakingly built into the treetops. We gazed at the waterfalls in the valley beneath. It was oh so pretty! There were flowers everywhere, and we were surrounded by trees on which lizards, songbirds and squirrels sat and scrambled. I was particularly excited to see an unusually brightly coloured bird which we failed to identify. I asked the waiter who told me it was a bulbul; we consulted the bird book which we always carried with us and found a picture of the red-whiskered bulbul. What a find. I was ecstatic!

As we walked back to the car through the garden, we saw many of the plants from our house in Hampton Wick. This really was bliss – a glimpse of heaven; a paradise on earth.

We drove on. Maggie curled up her feet and laid her head on Rusi's pillow positioned on my lap. Into Kerala – coconut land. After a while we stopped at a roadside café which was flying the Indian flag for Republic Day. We had our first thali – a selection of different dishes served in small bowls on a round tray. Maggie loved the curd and had seconds.

At 5 p.m. we arrived in Cochin. Oh dear, a terrible traffic jam... It is rush hour... Where do we go? Round and round, it seems. There were no hotels. Rusi was very quiet. It was very hard for him concentrating on the traffic and at the same time looking for suitable accommodation. We drove along the seafront, all to no avail. A mood of despondency crept in for the first time on the tour. Was our return to Cochin, which we remembered with such affection, a ghastly mistake? We stopped at an information centre which informed us that the Bulgatty Hotel, situated on a neighbouring island at which we stayed last time, was currently being refurbished. Anyway, we felt it was time to move on, to seek other accommodation: 'fresh woods and pastures new'*. In desperation, I asked about a guest house recommended by a dear friend, Bali, and received directions. It was some way away apparently, in Fort Cochin, which meant crossing two bridges.

We returned to the car. We came out like two sad old men, Maggie said later. We drove on in silence, asking the way many, many times. In India there are very few road signs, and there's a language problem too, because there are so many dialects, and the person who poses the question may well not understand or be understood by the person to whom the question is addressed. And the police are often bloody-minded and refuse to speak at all! Poor old Rusi, he drove heroically on and on and round and round, and all we could do was commiserate.

At last – a breakthrough. We found Kimansion, the guest house which Bali and Suresh had so warmly recommended. It was next door to Fort Heritage Hotel in a very salubrious suburb. The sea was nearby and there was an expanse of parkland on which the holidaying Indians were disporting themselves. Our spirits rose. Rusi and I entered the reception area while Maggie waited in agonised suspense. As we returned, all smiles, she was obviously greatly relieved. There was one snag, though. The rooms were very expensive, the last two rooms being available at £21 each. We decided to accept, as we were too tired to look elsewhere.

Our room in the garden was lovely. There was freshly laid coconut matting on the floor. There wasn't much furniture, but a super bed covered in white lace. There was

---

* From: Milton, John, *Lycidas*

an excellent loo and a shower tiled in blue. Our blue heaven! Bliss!

We had a quick shower and then went off to the hotel next door. Once settled at our table in the garden, we experienced a power cut, which is not unusual in India. A charming waiter brought us a torch. They are ready for such eventualities in India. We all had tomato soup, which was very good and then it started to rain. There was a huge thunderstorm with vivid lightning flashes. We were ushered into the dining room where we continued our meal.

I had a sizzling steak; Maggie had chicken laida, which proved disappointing, and Rusi had a fish curry. Maggie's meal was redeemed by a dish of good prawn rice.

For dessert she had pineapple slices, which she adores, and I had vanilla ice cream. Rusi tactfully declined. He was so good, as I am sure he felt we were overextending our budget. We were paying for everything for him this time – his accommodation and food. We felt we should, as he was such value. We could never contemplate a trip like this without his moral and active support.

The cost of the meal was £9.

We waded home through pools of water, the result of the thunderstorm. It was the first time we had experienced rain since we landed on Indian soil. The weather had been fabulous and we were gradually acquiring a tan.

Back in our room, the lights went out but only momentarily. A strange creature about three inches long was crawling up the bathroom wall, to Maggie's consternation. We called the gallant young manager, who identified the creature as a cockroach, and summarily shot it down with his spray gun. I read aloud a chapter of Anita Desai's *A Village by the Sea*, after which we contentedly fell asleep.

sunday, 28 january

Up to a breakfast of toast and tea in a large dining room with pictures of Jesus around.

A blue Ambassador car arrived and we were subjected to a terrible journey for an hour. The trip had been arranged by Rusi with the help of the young manager. Sitting alongside the driver, Rusi suffered in silence. Finally, in exasperation he told the driver to slow down, much to our relief.

At last we arrived at the appointed destination, where a guide was awaiting us. We walked amiably through green vegetation to a house and garden where the guide showed us a nutmeg tree.

Close by on the river was a rickety old boat which we all boarded. Rusi was ever present with an ever-helpful arm. He was so protective of us.

There followed an amazing morning travelling through intricate waterways. Our guide, Tambi, was great and recognised all the birds – two pied wagtails sitting on a log, one bee-eater, a cuckoo bird and numerous egrets.

Bushes and trees lined the riverbanks and Tambi identified them all: cashew nuts, wild pineapple, and loveliest of all, a yellow wild cotton flower which emulates the sun, rising in yellow and setting in red. Maggie was enthralled.

The boat was moored and we walked to a neighbouring village where we watched the local men making mats. Then on to a house, well constructed, where they made coir from the coconut with primitive machines. The women were lovely and friendly, balletic in their movements. Another two women whom we watched were making brooms for the house out of twigs: cottage industries.

A further walk revealed a woman making coconut mats. She looked very poor. She folded up the mat into a case space but we gently refused to buy. Her child begged a coin.

The village was so peaceful. Tambi explained that each village has a cooperative, a school, and a health centre. The villagers were mostly Hindu. The girls marry at eighteen; the men at twenty-one as a general rule. The average age at which people die is sixty-six. I was living on borrowed time!

We returned to our boat, which had been moored near a beautiful Keralan house. Back on board, Maggie had a biscuit and water, as her diabetic condition demanded. It was 11.15 a.m. We glided with an easy movement along such peaceful waters where we saw a great many egrets and blue kingfishers (rarities at home!).

Then came an unexpected stop. We stepped out of the boat and onto the shore where we drank coconut milk through a straw, and then the men chopped open coconuts for us.

And then the slow haul back, with the silent oarsmen pulling strongly and rhythmically upon their wooden oars. They spoke no English, but joined animatedly in the excitement when Maggie spotted a bird. Her excitement was infectious and was universally admired, but particularly in India where the people love her naïve, childlike appreciation of all things bright and beautiful, all creatures great and small. It is an endearing quality which I envy.

We loved the outing so much, so very much. The cost was 295 rupees each – about £11 altogether.

We said fond farewells to Tambi, who saw us back to our car. He was a wonderful guy, so quietly unassuming, and so knowledgeable.

We had a horrid drive back. The driver was mad. Thank God he wasn't driving us around on a permanent basis. Thank the Lord for Rusi, in whose safe hands we remained.

Back in Cochin, we decided to have lunch at the Malabar Hotel at the bottom of the road listed in the *Observer* and *Harper's Magazine* as one of the twenty best in India. We sat facing a classy grassy quadrangle at a table very close to a small pool with translucent blue water. Ideal for immersion, but not for swimming. Lunch was served: galette of potatoes and aubergine for me, ravioli for Maggie and green pea and cashew nut curry for Rusi – excellent. Plus two bottles of chilled water. Gorgeous!

After lunch, Rusi discreetly decided to leave us on our own, so Maggie and I seized the moment and sauntered to the beach. There was an impressive stone promenade, and many Indian families were making the most of the summer sun and strolling by the sea.

Maggie and I made a beeline for the Chinese fishing nets peculiar to this area. We watched for ages, fascinated, and Maggie 'clicked' like mad. 'Clicking' was the word Rusi used. We found it amusing and borrowed it on every possible occasion. It sounded more onomatopoeic than 'snapping' when associated with the camera. The crew, about six in all, hauled up the nets on a primitive pulley system using the local rocks to counterweight the catch. They pulled up the nets balletically every five minutes. In the large net the resultant catch looked ridiculously minute – one small fish every time.

'What's the name of the fish?' Maggie called to a smiling member of the crew.

'Mullet,' he replied.

It might be mullet, but not as we know it; looked more like a sardine.

We saw a boy taking up a basket of mullet to sell.

After a while, we paddled and then lay back on the sand for over an hour. So peaceful – such bliss!

As we were leaving the beach, a school party arrived. The girls waded into the water, screaming and fully clad.

Back to Room 105 at Kimansion, and we showered off the sand. I ordered tea and Rusi came to join us.

At 7 p.m. we walked down to the Malabar Hotel. Last night's puddles were gone. We had the same table facing a musical group positioned in the quadrangle.

We ordered two bottles of Kingfisher beer for the three of us. Maggie wrote to Sue, a close friend who lives in Buckinghamshire, and handed it over with other correspondence to the hotel reception for posting.

We had a simply marvellous meal. Maggie opted for fish: tuna mousse for starters, followed by snapper fish with masala spices, lovely veg – broccoli, rice and appa (Keralan rice cake); I had spaghetti à la Madhur Jaffrey, with an excellent tomato sauce; and Rusi had dal and rice. To follow, Rusi and I indulged ourselves in tiramisu. Scrumptious!

There was classical music throughout the meal. The group, comprising three men, played without a break. The instruments were varied: a violin, a rolled drum and an earthenware pot. The music was very plaintive, sad and haunting.

Looking around, it was a sumptuous scene: the assembled company being well dressed (Indian style) and there were many snooty English. It was very warm, and there were fairy lights everywhere.

Maggie pronounced the ladies loo excellent, and we were well satisfied with the proffered bill of £19 settled, for once, on Visa. It was, of course, well above budget, but we felt we needed a special treat at this stage of the journey.

We bade goodbye to the manager – a charming Mr Francis. He informed us that there were sixteen bedrooms ranging in price from £90 to £100, and we promised to return... 'To the restaurant, that is,' we muttered under our breath.

In the foyer we noted the headline on a national newspaper: 'Terrible earthquake in Gujarat – 16,000 killed'.

Rusi said quietly that Viraf's mother lived there. We would phone the children tomorrow and reassure them that the affected area was thousands of miles away. This had to be world news.

monday, 29 january

After a great sleep in a super bed we were up for breakfast – toast and tea. I paid the bill which amounted to 230 rupees for the two days.

We had a wonderful send-off from Sigu and Jose. They stood in the doorway and waved until we were out of sight. Maggie, who is more expressively emotional than I am, was very, very sad to leave. It had been a haven in the time of need, and those anxious moments when we arrived seemed very far away.

Refreshed, we enjoyed a glorious drive through Kerala. There were so many waterways, so many pretty women in multicoloured saris, and such an air of tranquillity. The tensions of London seemed so far away. Rusi solved all the problems, and there weren't many of those. We glided past beautiful Keralan houses. You could buy one for £10,000, according to Rusi. Every village we passed through appeared to have people celebrating something or other. Maggie 'clicked' a working elephant. I, with characteristic tardiness, failed to click another one, much to Maggie's annoyance.

On and on we went, past paddy fields with the customary egrets.

Lunch was taken at twelve o'clock. Rusi and I were unadventurous and opted for cheese sandwiches, while Maggie chose a masala omelette.

Imperceptibly the scenery changed as we climbed into the mountains. Maggie, who had kept her watch at English time ever since Heathrow, kept glancing at it. My watch supplied Indian time.

We are very anxious to contact Myf and reassure her that we were ok. The Gujarat earthquake made headline news and the victim toll was rising.

At 9.30 a.m. we found an STD telephone in a shack high up in the mountains. It was maintained by a woman in a red sari, along with her son.

We sat down in the back and dialled the number. It rang straight through! Wonderful! But would Myf be at her desk? I passed the receiver over to Maggie. Brilliant! She was there.

'Why haven't you phoned before?' said Myf crossly. Well, there's gratitude. What we didn't know was that the children had been very anxious about us for several days. The Gujarat Earthquake had been the number one item on the television news, and they were unsure of our where-abouts. Richard and Sue, friends of ours, were also worried about our safety, and Dafydd, our son, had phoned Ishver, a friend of the family, for reassurance.

Ishver had told Dafydd that India is a very large continent and that we were nowhere near the afflicted area. Maggie told Myf that we'd only heard about it last night, as we had been without newspapers and television sets; adding that we had contacted her at the first reasonable and appropriate time. Appeased, Myf listened to what Maggie had to say about the journey.

We told her that it was more wonderful here than ever. Myf was obviously delighted and wanted to know if we had asked Rusi if he was willing to take her and her husband, John, on a similar tour. 'Of course,' we replied.

They have been house-hunting with no success. 'Bring your deposit out here and buy a seashore house in Kerala,' we advised.

'Good idea,' said Myf. 'We'd like to open a wildlife centre in India.'

Back in the car, we agreed that it was gorgeous to hear her voice.

We arrived in Periyar at 4.30 p.m., weary after a very long drive in the sun. Following the recommendation of Bali and Suresh (yet again!) we drove into the Wildlife Sanctuary and headed for Periyar House. Rooms were available here but only for one night. The price worked out at £10 per person, so we readily accepted. The room was basic but OK. The loo was clean, but French i.e. a tiled hole in the ground.

We sat in the garden and took afternoon tea, while Rusi hared off to see his friend who managed a neighbouring hotel, still within the confines of the sanctuary. He returned in high spirits, having negotiated a room for us at £40 for the next night, as well as two free boat trips.

'You are our magic man,' said Maggie.

He said he'd sleep elsewhere. We sought reassurance that he'd be near and comfortable, and then concluded the deal. We'd had this arrangement on previous tours where the price of accommodation proved more than anticipated. On these occasions Rusi paid for himself. A friend indeed.

At 7.30 we met up again and repaired to a large dining room. It reminded Maggie of school. The food was served by a pleasant staff, buffet-style. We all had soup, fried rice, dal and bananas. Rusi and I had a delicious pineapple soufflé and plum cake. The food was very good, and all included in the price of the room. It was a pity we had to move the next day.

Bed followed at 9.30 p.m. I read another chapter of Desai, but Maggie slept fitfully because of a little lizard on the wall which made a racket throughout the night. *Chirrup! Chirrup!* I slept like a log – oblivious to it all!

tuesday, 30 january

I rose at 5.30 a.m. to shave. My hair was growing disgustingly long, as my reflection revealed. Down to the dining room for tea, supplemented by Hannah's diabetic biscuits.

Maggie, Rusi and I (we three!) walked briskly to the boat like children on a Sunday school outing, chattering animatedly like the monkeys in the branches above us. We learned that Rusi had booked us in to the top deck, and when the boat docked he forged ahead to get the front seats for us. What a man! What a queue-jumper! Once settled, we looked around and were dismayed to see how many white tourists there were – replete with expensive video cameras!

It was quite cold up on deck as there wasn't much sun. We saw masses of cormorants, several kingfishers and packs of wild dogs coming down to the water to drink. With their bushy tails, they looked more like foxes than dogs. Word went around that bison had been spotted on the hilltop. A charming Indian photographer and his girlfriend helped Maggie to identify three water otters and two snake birds.

It was a pleasant outing, but disappointing from a wildlife point of view. There was usually so much more to see. And worst of all, no elephants for Maggie.

A stroll back to Periyar House Hotel along a tree-lined road, for a delicious breakfast of cornflakes, omelettes and masala, toast and tea. This hotel cost us the princely sum of £30 for three (including dinner and breakfast). Not bad, eh?

Reluctantly, we packed up and moved next door (not

really – but nearly!) to the Aranya Nivas Hotel. Rusi had secured us a lovely room with a view of tall trees, plus a television set where we could see pictures of the Gujarat disaster – harrowing.

Next to the restaurant was a superb outside pool. Maggie and I love swimming and wasted no time in availing ourselves of the opportunity – straight in! It was very cold but lovely once you swam. We had great fun. The white latticed beds around the pool were so uncomfy – where, oh where, had the mattresses gone? We were plagued by ordinary flies – not, thank God, the horse variety. Maggie and I went upstairs and dressed for lunch. Rusi joined us, but not before Maggie checked her blood sugar count. The little machine revealed a figure of 7.3 and she was very thrilled.

Downstairs, the three of us consulted the menu and plumped unwisely for fish and chips; not a good choice. The service was poor, the head waiter positively grumpy – very unusual in India.

After a peremptory return to the pool, we gave up on the hardness of the latticed beds and the hordes of flies that plagued us, and retreated to our bedroom.

The bed upstairs was comfy and we napped happily for an hour or so. Such fun. Then we went down to the information centre. Apparently, according to the curator, we missed Hester the elephant, who had reported to the centre at 7.30 a.m. while we were out on the boat disappointedly looking for wildlife. Oh, the delicious irony of life!

We returned to our room and decided to pack our cases ready for an early start the next day. Then we watched the news headlines: 20,000 feared lost in earthquake.

Down to the dismal dining room, where there was a party of elderly persons. They looked so dull and hardly spoke. They were years older than ourselves, we concluded, in mind if not in fact.

The head waiter was equally dull. He gave the impression of favouring us with his presence. We had a good tomato soup (yet again – how dull can we get?). Dullness, like beauty is obviously in the eye of the beholder; then chicken Maryland with banana and pineapple, followed by slices of pineapple.

The indifferent quality of the meal was offset by the fact that we didn't have to pay for it: another perk arranged by Rusi. We raised our glasses of sealed mineral water to our absent friend – Rusi, the Magic Man.

Back in our room, we dimmed the lights and watched an Indian version of *Mastermind*. It was an exact copy. Three of the contestants were brilliant but the fourth was embarrassingly bad. Definitely the weakest link – goodbye and goodnight. Lights out!

Wednesday, 31 January

We awoke without the aid of the alarm clock at 8 a.m. On drawing the curtains I spied a lovely monkey sitting in a tree exactly opposite our third-storey window. Maggie quickly reached for her camera but on zooming in on him the camera surprisingly wound back at No. 11! She put in a new film. It went all right – and she crossed her fingers!

To breakfast, where we chatted to three people from Sri Lanka – an indigenous couple and a girl from Jamaica living in Canada. She had a fabulous video camera and showed Maggie a herd of elephants she'd seen from the boat yesterday. Apparently it was better to go on a boat in the afternoon if you wanted to see more animals. It was annoying to think we had the option of a free boat trip and chose to rest instead.

Rusi arrived three-quarters of an hour early. We went to the hotel post office and bought five cards at eight rupees apiece.

Off we went again on our travels with Mr B. There was a short stop in Periyar town to buy spices from a lovely boy who spoke fluent French. Maggie bought lots of spices, as they are very cheap in India.

There followed a very long journey through Tamil Nadu. It is not as beautiful as Kerala, and there are no wayside restaurants.

It was a grey cloudy day, one of the very few we experienced. At 7.15 p.m. British time we telephoned Hannah, our elder daughter, without success. Despondency crept in, and a subsequent feeling of *hiraeth* – a Welsh form of homesickness, but much worse!

We arrived in Trichy at 4.30 p.m., exhausted and depressed. However, we brightened up a little when Rusi found the Hotel Femina – a good hotel at a very reasonable price: £15 per room. The outdoor pool was one of the biggest and most attractive we had encountered in India.

Maggie was restless and wanted to see the Rock Temple, which our guidebooks singled out for praise. So off we went in search. Rusi didn't look too happy, but drove with characteristic stoicism. Just before dark we saw it, impressively silhouetted against the skyline. 'Tomorrow we'll go in,' said Rusi. Of course, we never did.

Rusi couldn't find the way back to the hotel. We drove round and round in silence. Despair set in and no one spoke. Depressed in the dark, we were totally lost and Rusi stubbornly refused to ask the way. Oh Rusi, where is your magic now? Wave your wand, boyo! Round and round the same familiar backstreets we went – and all to no avail. The Hotel Femina eluded us. One hour and fifteen minutes later we drove into the car park. Home at last! But what a tour of Trichy – its backstreets full of wooden and tin shacks and fragrant Indian smells.

It had been a dreadful day with very little food and drink to sustain us on the way.

Once in our room, Maggie and I showered together. Afterwards, we were joined by Rusi for a brandy in our room.

Feeling better, we went down for dinner, where Maggie discovered she had left her watch behind in the bedroom. I was feeling too tired to go back so I took the easy way and said it would be all right. Procrastination is a fault of mine. The dinner wasn't bad. There isn't more to say, but it cost £8.60.

When we returned to the bedroom the watch wasn't

there. Maggie swore she left it in the bathroom when we took the shower. But where was it now? We concluded it must have been stolen, and I felt as guilty as hell. Why on earth didn't I return to the room immediately when Maggie alerted me? She was very upset as the watch, minted for the *Buddy* first night, had a sentimental value; and not only that, she felt it was an intangible link with the children, set as it was at British time.

From time to time, she would look at the watch and imagine what the children were doing all those miles away; and now the link was gone. I felt dreadful. If only I had made the effort all this would not have happened. In a fit of despondent activity, I searched the room. For thirty minutes I looked. As I was on the point of admitting defeat I found it. Eureka! Where was it? You may well ask. Maggie had used it as a bookmark in one of the guidebooks. Relief reigned. Maggie felt that her link with the children had been restored and I felt exonerated. But oh, what a day!

Quietly relaxed once more, I read another chapter of Anita Desai's *A Village by the Sea* and we quickly fell asleep.

thursday, 1 february

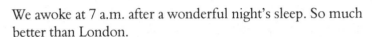

We awoke at 7 a.m. after a wonderful night's sleep. So much better than London.

We got up and went down to the pool. On the way we saw Rusi watching a boy washing our car. The pool was empty but a boy was cleaning it with a vacuum cleaner. After anxious moments of negotiation, we agreed to use half the swimming area. What a relief! 'For this relief, much thanks!' Oh, the joy of swimming in warm water beneath a cloudless sky. It was glorious. There was only us swimming; no other people about except Rusi, who took time off from supervising the cleaning of his car to check that we were all right.

Later we had a huge breakfast in a dark coffee room. Why do they have curtains drawn in so many coffee shops? If they lived in England they wouldn't exclude the sun. Maggie had huge puris with chutney and then joined me in a continental breakfast of toast and jam and pineapple slices, with lime soda to drink. Rusi had a lovely onion dosa. Aware of yesterday's food shortage, and Maggie's diabetic condition, Rusi thoughtfully arranged for a takeaway pack of cheese sandwiches to be consumed en route.

After breakfast I paid the bill: £26 for two rooms. Ours was £15. Very good! As I was standing in the foyer I saw – I swear I saw – a mongoose mount the stairs, heading for the first floor. I told Maggie and she queried me with a disbelieving smile… Pink elephants next, I wonder? But I swear I saw it. It was just like the one we saw behind the rocks in Fort Cochin.

Off at 10.15 a.m., with happy memories of Trichy after an extremely dodgy start. Feeling that fortune had finally favoured us, we drove happily along. It was a difficult journey through busy towns.

At 7.15 a.m. on Maggie's watch we stopped outside an STD shack and telephoned Hannah. Better luck this time. She was there, and we had a gloriously animated chat, liberally interspersed with clichés. All was well. Megan – our dog – was fine; Hannah's new post as team manager was fine. We told her that we were fine and the weather likewise. She responded by telling us that the weather was awful, cold and wet; and that she and Paul, her partner, were going to the cottage next weekend. As we speak I can picture the cottage – our little idyllic primitive home in Wales with its ingle nook and timbered beams – and *hiraeth* returns once more. A young boy working on a commission basis gratefully accepted our £2 as we left.

On we went once more. Maggie consumed her doggy bag after a stop for tea in a hideous Tamil Nadu hotel. The very name is synonymous with dirt and noise and all things unpleasant. And this hotel was one of the weakest links in the dubious chain. It was so dirty – the cups, the table, the loo. How could they? We travelled along pleasant roads by paddy fields peopled with egrets.

At long last we turned off for Pondicherry after seeing a large group of pilgrims in orange and green walking to a temple. This had been a familiar sight on our previous visit three years ago. This time there were some women – barefooted, like the men, as an act of penance. We saw a group at the river, washing, watched over by the effigy of a Hindu god carried on a cart.

The entrance of Pondicherry town is invitingly captivating, but the town itself is busy. We saw the Hotel Anandha where we'd stayed last time. We sensed that Rusi would like to go back, though he didn't say a word.

We drove along the sea front to the Ashram Guest House and Rusi, pale and strangely muted, sent Maggie and myself in first. The reason soon became obvious. The boys on the desk were quite fierce and looked arrogantly at Rusi. We, as tourists with passports, were welcome. But what about Rusi? They enquired, 'Is he a friend or a driver?' They gestured towards him to take a back seat.

'A friend,' we chorused.

'A friend of ten years,' Maggie exaggerated.

'And a respected businessman,' I added.

They scrutinised him and Rusi sat uncomfortably awaiting their response. They then interrogated him as if he were a spy. Rusi looked pale and uncomfortable and was obviously under considerable strain.

'No liquor, no noise,' they warned, looking at Rusi.

At last, he was approved, subsequently being bound over conditional on his behaviour, we felt. Poor Rusi, he deserved better than this, but we did want the rooms, and we felt the accommodation would ultimately be worth the humiliating experience. And we were right. Rusi was accepted. The boys relaxed and Rusi smiled at last.

We were shown a cottage for 600 rupees and another for 500 rupees, Numbers 7 and 8. Ours was Number 7, with 'gentleness' written above the door.

The rooms were basic but they were on the ground floor facing a beautiful garden, and the sound of the sea was marvellous.

Approved and composed once more, Rusi our friend brought his car in and our cases were carried to our rooms. Maggie told the young men in reception that Sri Aurobindo, whose ashram this was and whose picture adorned the wall, had attended our son Dafydd's school, St Paul's, and later they both went to King's College. They were most impressed.

A quick trip to the restaurant followed, with all the

windows opening on to the sea and the rocks below. It was so wonderful. The sound and smell of the sea rejuvenated our noses and our ears. We love the sea, and we particularly loved this blue, blue sea as it pounded upon the rocks.

We ordered tea and cinnamon toast. Rusi didn't look his usual happy self. I hoped he wouldn't continue to feel uncomfortable. Gradually, however, the peace and congeniality of the place began to take over.

At 6 p.m. we left for the ashram by car. It was just the same as we remembered it, with glorious flowers everywhere. The shrine was covered in flowers, particularly jasmine and rose petals. Maggie lingered at the shrine, touching the flowers and giving personal thanks to Mother, whose cheerful image smiled upon us everywhere. She stayed long after Rusi and I had returned to sit on the stone steps. There was a sacred stillness that had lasted for many years. We felt the positive presence of goodness, of reflection and prayer. There was a piety which persisted and purified the soul. It was a very moving experience to be part of this pilgrimage.

When we came out, Rusi went to the car while Maggie and I wandered down the street. He warned us not to go into the Temple; we wondered why. Maggie was delighted to see a working elephant giving blessings at the gate for money. There was not much to see – a few paltry stalls – so we sauntered back to the car.

We saw a woman in white – white shorts, white top and white turban – and we wondered if it was the uniform dress of Mother's devotees.

Maggie asked her where we should eat and she recommended the Hotel Anandha, much to Rusi's obvious delight.

We went there immediately and when Rusi parked the car we were greeted by men in turbans who were waiting at the door. They were just as we remembered them, and so was the hotel. The little jewellery boutique in the foyer still had the jewelled elephant I wanted to buy last time for £200. It was exquisite but I still couldn't afford it. Next time, maybe…

The food was disappointing last time, but this time we had a super vegetarian meal: aubergine and cashew nuts, asparagus in cheese sauce, tagliatelle and tomato biryani with iced water. Excellent value for £8 for three.

Home, Rusi! There was such peace in our garden. We listened to the sea from bed as our contented eyelids closed. Maggie wanted another night there.

Maggie and Dinu in The Garden of Allah

Rusi with 'his boys'

'We three' at the Renaissance Hotel in Bangalore

Wash day at the hotel

Govinder at the bird sanctuary at Shrirangapatnam

The long marble table at Bamboo Banks Farm

Two happy dinner guests!

A wild boar at Bandipur National Park

At the elephant farm

Room 101 – the haunted room!

Rusi at the wheel

A happy two with Rusi

The spice boys!

The Chinese fishing nets

Anyone for coconuts?

There are egrets everywhere in Southern India – well, usually!

Maggie in the gardens of the Ashram Guest House in Pondicherry

The Rock Temple at Trichy

Rock carvings at Mahabalipuram

The pool at the Ideal Resort in Mahabalipuram

Lakshmi and her sister

Classical dancers at Mahabalipuram

Maggie 'clicks' a working elephant

A common sight in India

A street in Puttaparthi

A gateway to Sai Baba's ashram

Sai Baba's Hospital in Puttaparthi

A household shrine to Sai Baba

friday, 2 february

We awoke at 7 a.m. and strolled across the garden to look at the sea. Counting my remaining rupees, I realised that we would probably need more before we reached Bangalore next week. At all events, I realised that if I didn't change more traveller's cheques it would be a close-run thing. Maggie, who was more cautious than I am about such matters, suggested that with the international community here in Pondicherry, it would be easier to change money now rather than in Mahabalipuram, our next destination. So it was decided and I asked the boys at the desk to recommend a 'cambio' which they obligingly did. It was only a few streets away and easily walkable, they said.

Rusi joined us and we went in to breakfast. Over breakfast, consisting of wholemeal toast, omelette and coffee for under a £1, Rusi informed us that he now loved the place and wanted to bring Dinu here. He met some people from Bangalore on an early morning stroll and now felt totally accepted. Rejection time was over; the battle was won for him. It was good to see his confidence returning.

Rusi and I walked into town to get the money while Maggie stayed behind, contentedly reading *Country Living*, which Myf gave her before we left England, a long, long time ago. Maggie looked so well and happy as we breezed into town.

The recommended 'cambio' was excellent, and I arranged the transaction with ease and goodwill. Three

Marks and Spencer's traveller's cheques yielded approximately 20,000 rupees.

Three cheerful people set off for Auroville and we arrived there by 12.30 p.m. after an obligatory stop in the woods. We went to the restaurant immediately. Maggie, who was feeling poorly, had a cheese roll and tea while Rusi and I sampled a lassi. I love a lassi – preferably mango!

Afterwards we went to an exhibition of sculpture and then to the shop where we bought necklaces, writing paper (for Colleen, our daughter-in-law), incense sticks, pretty little vanity bags and a bendy toy for Dafydd's desk; we spent £11 in all.

After that we watched a video on Auroville – a democratic, self-supporting, international community founded by Mother from Pondicherry. We noticed on the video that there were no old people, and were somewhat disconcerted. The community comprised 15,000 at that present moment but they hoped for 50,000. There was good health care. On the way out, Maggie asked an Aurovillian if there were any old people.

'Yes,' he replied. 'One is eighty-six and there are fifty over seventy.' So there we were – we could join, if the committee voted us in.

At 4 p.m. Rusi drove us to the Matrimandir, to the crystal which is the heart of Auroville.

The car park was busy; full of buses. Manifold notices around the place instructed us to leave any bags and cameras in the car. The tour was unfriendly, matched by the attitude of the stewards, of whom there were far too many. To justify their presence, they checked our passes every twenty yards.

Near the Matrimandir, we had to take off our shoes and leave any water containers. The stewards were very bossy, and contradicted the very essence of Mother's love philosophy. They looked suspiciously at everyone, scowling all the time.

The dome was vast; its exterior was covered in gold panels, but not completely by any means. In fact it was only half finished. Three years before, Rusi had said it would be finished shortly. How wrong can you be? Sai Baba, who can set up and complete hospitals in months should be given the tender.

The climb was difficult, particularly for Maggie, who was still feeling poorly. Rusi was most solicitous. We climbed and climbed for ages. The building reminded Maggie of the National Theatre, she told me later. It was the concrete, I suppose. She couldn't confide her thoughts till later as we were sworn to silence, and the stewards were there to impose the law. Woe betide the garrulous! The looks of those stewards could kill!

At last we could see a green crystal in the roof. It looked beautiful but not as large as we expected. A disappointment, really, after all the security and hype. We were afforded a glimpse, not a sit-down hour of meditation, as we had fondly imagined.

I looked at Maggie. We made eye contact and giggled, thinking of Myf's reaction to this silent pilgrimage.

Down, down we went past more stewards, reclaimed our sandals and moved in silent contemplation back towards the car park from whence we came. Through the lovely gardens we went, without a word.

Rusi rushed on ahead to prepare the car for Maggie. He was worried that the whole expedition may have exhausted her.

Once in the car, en route to Pondicherry, we discussed the crystal. Rusi liked it but I had to confess I found the imposed silence too long. It was counterproductive, and induced an air of levity. Maggie was even more outspoken and she voiced her feelings in the 'suggestions' book at the Auroville Information Centre. She wrote of the Matrimandir experience, 'Totally non-spiritual, too many officials – men and bureaucracy gone mad. Mother wouldn't approve.' She signed it, 'Maggie Harries Williams'.

Back at Pondicherry, Rusi stopped in a basement café called 'Salt and Pepper' for Maggie to have a cup of tea and a toasted cheese sandwich – 55 rupees in all. The price was good, but the café wasn't.

Back to our lovely cottage. I was called outside by Rusi to see a mongoose on the lawn. He suggested we should close our front door. This was our third encounter with a member of the mongoose family on the holiday. I had seen one walking up the stairs at the Hotel Femina in Trichy, and both Maggie and I saw one on the beach at Fort Cochin. Are they mongeese or mongooses in the plural? Hmmm…

We sat on the veranda and watched it grow dark.

Dinner time; so we repaired once again to the Hotel Anandha restaurant for a vegetarian meal similar to the one we had enjoyed last night. There were more people in the restaurant tonight, and the atmosphere was congenial. Immediately behind us was an extrovert young American and his Japanese girlfriend. His accent reminded us of 'Bri Bri', an old and valued friend from Key West.

We were back and in bed by 9.45 p.m. I read another chapter from *A Village by the Sea*. It was a sad episode tonight. Mother was dying and the Magic Man duped the children who sought his help in desperation. I put down the book, whereupon Maggie had an attack of heartburn. It was agony for a moment. Thankfully there was Alka-Seltzer in the medicine bag, and Maggie eventually dropped off to sleep.

Saturday, 3 February

Maggie woke and declared herself fit. Then, to prove the point, she went off to collect our laundry. Twenty-one articles for 115 rupees – about £1.60 in all – amazing! And beautifully done.

We had a good breakfast in our stunning little canteen. There were superb views of the sea through every window.

While Maggie waited, I went to reception to ask if we could stay another night, and to our mutual delight I learnt that we could. So it was three nights in Pondicherry – not the scheduled two.

Today had been designated a day of rest and relaxation, so we read more Desai till noon – on cream plastic chairs on the veranda!

A well-equipped army of young cleaners swooped down upon us, poised to clean the cottage if we so wished. We gave the idea our approval, and Maggie handed out sweets, which were gratefully accepted by the bevy of giggling girls.

We opted for a meal on site, and at breakfast we ordered a lunch – a delicious thali for forty-five rupees. It was so tasty and so ridiculously cheap.

We slept on our beds for two hours in the afternoon, lulled by the sound of the sea. Oh, what peace! What bliss! It was so very wonderful here. The room was full of gentle vibes produced by years of prayer. There was such an atmosphere of joyful tranquillity. Mother smiled down from the wall.

Over for tea in the canteen, and then off to the ashram. We parked outside the bookshop, and we bought books written by the Mother and picture postcards of her.

Down the street was the ashram and it was there we wended our way. Such peace, and lovely flowers! We meditated beneath the frangipani tree which loftily dominated the shrine.

On our return ride to the guest house, we passed a large restaurant. It is called 'Le Club' and is housed in a spacious colonial residence built when the French, under Governor Dupleix, ruled in Pondicherry. His statue stands on the promenade near where we were staying.

The restaurant was comfortably full – a tribute to the cooking, which deserves the highest praise. The menu was rather special for this part of the world and we chose tomato soup, seer fish and *frites* replete with mushroom sauce.

Lemon crêpe followed for Maggie, and I introduced Rusi to crème brûlée. Total cost: £12.50. Worth every rupee, I'd say. We shook hands with the chef (an Indian trained in French cuisine) and with all the staff, and bade goodnight to a Canadian couple (mother and daughter seated at the next table).

On leaving the restaurant we tried to phone Myf and Dafydd with no success. They were either out or engaged.

Not to worry! We returned to our garden and sat by the sea. We were very sad to leave and Maggie confided that a part of her would stay in Pondicherry for ever.

We went to the reception to collect our key and talk to the young man at the desk. He was a pharmacist by profession, from Madras University, but he was now working for the Organisation. He worked for Boots until it was taken over by a German firm and he was made redundant. He told us you could fly to Madras from London and hire a taxi to Pondicherry – they'd send one from the guest house.

Maggie smiled. She was reassured and now knew she'd return.

We went to bed and listened. All was peaceful now – just the sound of the sea and the bullfrogs!

sunday, 4 february

After another excellent night's sleep, we woke at 8 a.m. Maggie reflected sadly that we had to move on. We loved Pondicherry – both the ashram and the guest house. Maggie opened the window for a final look at the sea and the palm trees; then dashed off to the laundry man to pick up yesterday's laundry! Four articles for twenty-one rupees – even the knickers were ironed! On her way back she encountered the man on the gate who had greeted us so cordially for the past few days and told him that we were going – reluctantly.

At 9 a.m. we had a huge breakfast at our customary table near the window. Pineapple and yoghurt, poached egg and toast for Maggie. Rusi and I had omelette. Then we all had coffee.

It took us ages to pack. Our heart wasn't in it! We said goodbye to reception as we handed in our keys. We thanked the lady in charge for making our stay so perfect. She was charming, and said, 'The guest house is for lovely people like you.'

Then we joined our cases in the car and drove out of the gates for the very last time.

Maggie had a clutch of cards which she needed to post so we went to a funny little post office, tucked away in the backstreets. It was very busy and extremely dark. Fortunately, there was a separate section for stamps. There were three post boxes which all looked equally unlikely. Would Maggie's postcards ever reach their destination?

Who knew? Here goes! Eeny, meeny, miney mo!

One last visit to the ashram. Maggie wanted to ask Mother to ensure another journey here. She was desperately keen to return. We walked past the women who sat outside, selling flowers for the ashram; gift offerings for the shrine. There weren't many pilgrims there that morning. They tended to favour the afternoons. One last trip to the bookshop to buy a picture of Mother for Colleen and a sticker for the Capri, and then we were off. Going, going, gone! *Au revoir* Pondicherry. We will return!

There followed a brilliant rural drive to Mahabalipuram along the coastal road. This road was new since our last visit, and it traversed rich agricultural land. There was an affluent air to the area. The red-brown earth was beautiful and the prolific paddy fields were dotted with a multitude of egrets.

But where, oh where, had the paddy birds gone? They were a popular sight last time.

A bathroom stop was needed, so Maggie and I crouched in the undergrowth beside a huge well and a tethered bullock. Rusi never failed to find us a spot far from the madding crowd.

Unfortunately there were no restaurants on this road and the only break was a bathroom stop which Maggie and I needed.

However, the journey only took two hours, so we were OK. We drove to our old hotel – Golden Resort – and Rusi and I investigated. The price of our old cottage had increased to £20; it was still available. There were, in fact, many unoccupied rooms. The place looked more run-down than I remembered and Rusi too was unimpressed.

We left the reception without committing ourselves, and decided to try our luck at the Ideal Resort a mile or two further on.

The manager here was a friend of Rusi – yet again! Rusi

generally managed to have influence in high places at the right time. His friend said there was one room for £20. I looked at it with Rusi and we were both very impressed. It was stunning! I definitely wanted it. Rusi said he'd happily stay elsewhere – a fair indication that this room was good value for us. Maggie came from the car, took one look and clinched the deal. She declared Room 22 wondrous. She was particularly happy with the large balcony from which she could see the sea over the hotel's restaurant – all together an enchanting view.

Having decided on our accommodation for the next four nights, we drove into the town. En route we had to pay a 20p toll. The object of the journey was food so we headed for the Hotel Veelas, where we had a thali and an onion dosa. The restaurant was as good and congenial as we remembered it.

Mahabalipuram was a favourite of ours on our last journey three years ago. Our meal was very economical – £2.20 – and very filling.

Back at our hotel, Rusi left us, and Maggie and I unpacked. As we'd be here for four nights, we decided to put everything away, using all the available drawer and wardrobe space. What a luxury! Oh, we do like to be beside the seaside – and for four days! Unbelievable!

We lay down on the bed for an hour, and then got up to sample the pool. 'The best ever' was Maggie's verdict, and I agreed. It was a good size, deep and warm. What bliss!

The swim over, we withdrew to our room and had a pot of coffee brought to us which we drank on the balcony. It cost thirty-five rupees. I gave the boy ten rupees as a tip. I knew it was overtipping, but who cares? Damn it, I was happy! In joyful mood, we dressed for dinner.

Rusi joined us. He'd found himself reasonable accommodation at the Golden Resort. He had special driver's rates and was perfectly happy. The prevailing mood was one of contentment, and we animatedly recalled the day's exploits with a great deal of glee.

Maggie sampled the prawns but was disappointed to find them overcooked. I had fish and chips and Rusi had vegetable balls. The bill amounted to £9 which was expensive but the ambience was perfect.

monday, 5 february

Rusi wasn't due at breakfast, but at 8.45 a.m. there he was. Maggie and I had a superb swim at 8 a.m after quite a good night's sleep, but we didn't like the mosquito net. It looked pretty, but it restricted our nocturnal movements. The noise of a bird in the roof above us was also a little inhibiting!

We had a full buffet breakfast, by accident rather than design. Maggie felt we should have had a choice, but we didn't. A case of all or nothing at all. In the event it proved good value for money – 150 rupees for very good porridge, omelette, fruit juice and fruit etc.

Off to Mahabalipuram for a sightseeing tour. First stop: the Shore Temple. We had a shock in store. On 20 October last year, the entry fee went up to 10 rupees for Indians and 455 rupees for foreigners. We hated that connotation and were horrified by this act of fiscal discrimination. We decided not to go in for £12 as we had many pictures. Interestingly, we observed that there were no foreigners inside the Shore Temple compound. We were all outside the wire netting, peering in. After one or two minutes we moved off and sought out the beach in order to view the temple from the other side. The beach was crowded and there were lots of children swimming from filthy sands.

Time to move on to Aranja's Penance, with its marvellous rock carvings – primarily of elephants. They were superb. The only trouble was that we were continually harassed by hawkers selling postcards and small, carved elephants. They wouldn't leave us alone. Quiet contemplation of this superb seventh century work of art was impossible, so reluctantly we moved on.

The next port of call was the lighthouse, which necessitated a challenging climb. Rusi waited below in the shade. We were harassed once more, but this time by beggars, who offered for our perusal nothing more than their appalling mutilations. The sight was heart-rending. But where do you start, and to whom do you give? If you proffer money to one they gather like birds in quest of food, squabbling around you desperate for alms.

There was peace at the top and a wonderful view. Maggie chatted to a cheery group of Indians who were on an office outing from Madras – a day trip. It was obvious that they had a harmonious relationship and were happy to spend time with one another, even on Sunday. Maggie offered to take a group photograph and earned a spontaneous cheer and round of applause in delighted gratitude. It was not so peaceful now but there was a happy holiday spirit which nearby children and monkeys seemed to share.

On the way down, I saw a blind beggar with no hands and my stony heart melted. I gave him money and he beamed in gratitude. I couldn't begin to imagine his problems.

On to the Hotel Veelas for dosas and pineapple juice. Refreshed, we wandered a little in the main street and chanced upon a lovely little shop run by a charming young man, from whom we bought two Kodak films for 210 rupees. This is about £1.50 per film and in England they cost over £4. How can they? Rusi said the films are manufactured in India but, even so, how can they justify such a price differential? We also bought four postcards at 5 rupees each.

Across the road we saw a tailor's and wandered in out of curiosity, though Maggie wanted to buy some outfits in

India, I was sure. She ordered a cotton kurta in a beautiful shade of purple for £6. The tailor took quick measurements and promised to make it by tomorrow. It might be Sunday, but this was no day of rest for him.

We were back at the pool by 1 p.m., where we spent a happy afternoon swimming and reading.

Then we strolled along the beach to see the local fishing boats. They are so primitive in design and construction. They scarcely seemed seaworthy, being simply planks of wood tied together with yellow rope. While we were looking at the boats, a pretty young girl in a grey dress came up and asked us a lot of personal questions about ourselves. 'Is this your husband?' She went to the local school and was as bright as a button. She told us her name was Lakshmi and she lived nearby.

At 7 p.m. Rusi arrived. Maggie looked stunning in black. Down we went to dinner and were entertained throughout the meal by two Indian musicians playing in classical style. We were a very appreciative audience and we helped to lead the applause from time to time. The food was equally enjoyable. Maggie had fish and chips (seer fish, of course!). I had aloo gobi, and Rusi tried the Chinese fried rice. The bill: £7. India is a country where you are never afraid to pick up the tab.

We finished eating at about ten o'clock, so decided to go into Mahabalipuram to phone the children and Geraint, her brother. Looking at my watch upside down – the watch, that is, not me – I saw that it would be about 4.30 in Wales, and Maggie, consulting her own chronometer, confirmed this. We found a well-run kiosk with a helpful young man and had the good fortune to find Geraint in. He told us that Hannah and Myf were in the cottage with Paul and John. They watched the international rugby match between England and Wales on the television yesterday at Ger's. England thrashed Wales, but we won't go into that. Geraint was delighted to speak with us, but he always sounds a little awestruck when we telephone from abroad. Next we phoned Dafydd and got his news. It was lovely to hear his voice. Total cost – 151 rupees. Excellent value.

On returning to the hotel we discovered that the musicians were still there, so we had a pot of tea, listening to the music. It was so peaceful and we were very happy.

On the way up to our room we meet the hotel manager, Mr Francis, who was so charming. He kept a strict eye on everything but in the most pleasant manner: the 'hands-on' policy.

tuesday, 6 february

After an excellent sleep, we rose at 8 a.m. I shaved and Maggie did the laundry; routine chores. And then to the pool. It was such a luxury – a large pool to ourselves. It was exactly the kind of thing that we dreamt about in England.

Then to breakfast, feeling fit and contented. We ate and ate. Large porridge, glasses of pineapple juice, masala dosas, rolls and cheese etc.

Stuffed, we drove to Tiger Caves, where there are carved rocks of Hindu origin dating back to the seventh century. The pillared building is imbued with awe-inspiring spirituality and Maggie sat in silent meditation. There were very few people and no one disturbed the peace. The presence of a pied wagtail – elegant in movement – intruded upon my abstract mood. In our own time, we left this beautiful stone edifice and moved on. Twenty metres away we found a huge natural phallic rock. Highly unusual and very impressive. I took a photograph of Maggie and Rusi in front of it. Then on to another spectacular building, which Maggie had named Richie's Temple three years ago, for it was here that Maggie sensed his spiritual presence soon after his untimely death. It was a most moving experience. Now, in February 2001, Maggie felt that Richie Warwick was at peace.

Maggie and I walked up to a nearby hut. The latticed door was locked so we peered in and saw six heads of Hindu gods garlanded with flowers. It was an unforgettable sight. Everywhere we looked there were signs that personal worship had taken place, and evidence remained in the ashes circled by stones. Wistfully, we returned to the car and encountered a noisy group of students arriving in a coach. Their whoops of delight and banter contaminated the surrounding serenity. It was, of course, only harmless fun, but we were glad we'd arrived before them and enjoyed our moments of quiet contemplation.

We drove on to the market place to the constant Indian bustle and activity, and then to the Five Raithu. This is another historic monument wired off at a prohibitive price to the foreigner. We peered in at a distance as we had done yesterday, envious of the Indians who had a close-up view for only ten rupees. £8 per tourist was too much. We learned later that the locals were apparently sympathetic to our cause, and had actually organised an unsuccessful strike to stop the new fiscal legislation from coming into force.

Finally, Maggie could not resist the persistent purveyors of merchandise who crowded round us all the time. After much good-natured haggling she purchased a jade elephant from a pleasant youth for 100 rupees. Rusi felt we might do better in the shops, so he took us to one nearby. Maggie, in her element, struck a hard bargain with a po-faced man who agreed, somewhat reluctantly, to part with two elephants for 100 rupees. He was not pleased!

On our way out of the town we stopped at the tailor's to collect Maggie's purple kurta. It fitted perfectly. I handed over the promised £6 and we all declared ourselves happy with the deal.

Back to the hotel, and we ran to the poolside where we had reserved our beds with towels earlier in the day. Rusi resisted our entreaties to join us in the pool. He always said he would tomorrow, but of course, he never did.

At 4.30 p.m. we decided to go to the beach, as we felt in need of sand and sea. We wandered through the extensive green grounds of the hotel, past the cottages until we reached the wicker gate which led onto the golden sand. The sea was really too rough to swim in, so I amused myself by sitting on the edge and being buffeted by the waves. What a glorious way to spend a happy hour in the sun! Maggie meanwhile was using her bargaining skills to obtain a bright yellow bedspread for Hannah. As I approached they were settling the deal, and the vendor was highly amused by the whole proceedings. Maggie has a knack of turning the serious tedious business of commerce into an enjoyable game. The man had obviously never met a woman like her before, and signalled to me by the look on his face how lucky I was to have such a woman as a partner. And, of course, I am. He was such a jolly man.

The business transaction concluded, we repeated yesterday's stroll to the fishing boats further along the shore. The children, fresh out of school, came running towards us performing cartwheels for our amusement and admiration. Lakshmi, in a grubby school uniform, was among them. They were such lovely children, with an enchanting mixture of innocence and guile. They were eager for pens but we hadn't got any with us. We promised them tomorrow as we left them on the shore.

Back to the hotel and to our room, where we shared a pot of tea on the balcony and we watched darkness fall over the sea and listened to the fishing boats going out. Such quiet communion with nature. Elsewhere in the towns at this hour the hustle and bustle of the daily traffic would be unbearably noisy.

> For thy peace, O Lord, we give our grateful thanks.
> The day thou gavest now is ended.
> The darkness falls at thy behest.[1]

---

[1] John Ellerton, 'The Day Thou Gavest, Lord, Is Ended', 1870

At seven o'clock Rusi arrived. 'Twas the hour of Rusi, and at 7.30 p.m. after a nip of brandy and a few nibbles from the old country, we repaired to the poolside where the tables were laid out so prettily, bedecked with fairy lights. There was an air of carnival and of light-hearted merriment, though many of the tourist tables seemed out of tune with the harmonious surroundings. Some people, it would appear, are never happy; and there were mild disputes over the ownership of misappropriated chairs. But there we are! The food was laid out on trestle tables, buffet-style, under winking lights, and the blue water of the pool sparkled. We made a very happy trio. As we joined a leisurely queue for our plates to be filled, we were given jasmine garlands by the manager.

We had intended to eat elsewhere tonight – in the town – but the manager had arranged for classical dancers to perform on a raised dais in the grassy gardens after the meal, and of course we were loath to miss the opportunity of witnessing such a spectacular event in the open balmy air.

Rusi only ate the main course and left before the dance. There must have been a good film on television. We paid 375 rupees for his ticket too! Ah well!

After the meal we gathered on the lawn in front of the dais and watched the dancers performing classical myths, aided by musicians and a narrator. She was the same woman we had seen three years ago. The troupe of five dancers performed with agility and skill. One was a child of dubious sexuality: the granddaughter or grandson of the narrator we surmised.

They projected great joy and happiness, with their eyes and teeth flashing like winking lights mirrored in the pool. Their fingers and wrists moved with the dexterity of magicians as we sat in a circle around them. The pièce de résistance was a snake dance performed with unbelievably lithe sinuosity. The programme lasted an hour and the little group of performers were applauded vigorously at the end.

We were back in our room at 10.30 p.m., but were no sooner settled in the bed for our nocturnal slumbers when the phone rang. Who on earth could want to speak to us in a foreign clime at this untimely hour? Our hearts raced! The children were in trouble... Surely not! They didn't know where we were. Or could it be Rusi, to tell us he must return to Bangalore to drive Viraf to Gujarat? In the event, it was none of these wild, disturbing speculations. It was the laundry department informing us that our order was ready for delivery. 'Not now,' we said, in a mixture of relief and annoyance, 'tomorrow will do.'

My tummy wasn't too good so I took a Beechams powder once again.

Hypochondriac that I am, I was convinced it was the onset of malaria! I told Maggie that I might die in the night.

wednesday, 7 february

At 8 a.m. prompt, the laundry department phoned and then came round with eleven articles for 59p. If only we could have the same service in England for the same price!

Swam, and to breakfast. We told Rusi to come at eleven allowing Maggie time to write her letters. True to form, he arrived at ten o'clock but we still didn't leave until 11 a.m. for the post office. Once again it was a shack and there was a lengthy queue. We paid eight rupees to send the postcards and fifteen rupees for the letters.

Maggie felt we still needed more elephants, as they made very useful presents. Rusi drove us to an appropriate shop, and Maggie went through her familiar bargaining routine until the very charming woman agreed to sell us four elephants for 2,00 rupees.

In buoyant mood, we crossed the road and entered a small silk shop. The girl in there was called Ganthera and came from Gujarat. She said her brother made most of the items on display in the shop, though she called it a 'boutique'. She was a very pretty girl and very sweet natured. Maggie obviously liked her but was still relentlessly ruthless in the pursuit of a bargain: no quarter given. A wall hanging originally priced at 550 was finally sold at 200 rupees, and an elephant frieze for above the door became Maggie's property for 180 rupees, as did three scarves for 250 rupees.

Maggie was on form that morning. She loves a good haggle.

Back to the hotel we went, happy with our purchases. Rusi departed and we lay in the hot noonday sun by the pool – the 'mad dogs' syndrome!

We ordered tomato and cheese sandwiches and a pot of tea for lunch. We spent the next few hours sunbathing, then cooling off in the water. Maggie spent a lot of time in a large black tyre ring in the middle of the pool. As I wasn't feeling too good – malaria is hell! – I slept a little and consequently felt much better.

At four o'clock we roused ourselves and sauntered to the beach. The security guard – a huge man with smile to match – offered us two chairs. He saw a pen in my pocket and asked if he could have it. What is this obsession with pens? We asked Rusi one day. Why do they want them? And Rusi sagely replied that it wasn't so much the pen itself but the action of giving and receiving that motivated the requests. It was a token of friendship. With this in mind I parted with the pen.

The customary beach vendors approached us and Maggie purchased two scarves for seventy-five rupees. We were shown a beauty with sequined pearls on royal blue, for which he asked 750 rupees. Maggie for once resisted the challenge and failed to put in a counter bid. She had bargained enough for one day.

Later we saw the scarf changing hands and Maggie harboured regrets. If only…

We sat and read for a while but then we saw the boats were getting ready to journey out to sea, so we walked along the beach to gain a closer look.

Then, who should we see but Lakshmi coming to claim her pen. 'You promised yesterday…,' she began and could scarcely believe her luck when she was presented with the object of her desire. This, or course, started a flood of requests from all the children.

'Pen! Pen! Pen!'

Like the tennis stars at Wimbledon who sign the auto-graph books of the lucky few, so Maggie dispensed pens which she had brought from England for this very purpose, until the supply ran dry. It is better to give than to receive, I say – any day!

Maggie took her camera and wandered off to the fishing boats for a permanent record of this nightly ritual. She loved to watch the boats setting out to sea.

Back to the pool at five o'clock where we meet a charming couple from Yugoslavia. Funny to hear their native land described as Yugoslavia; it has an old-fashioned ring – a reminder of the days when Tito ruled supreme. In actual fact they came from Belgrade in Serbia, but that had unpleasant memories of bombings and Milosovich and ethnic cleansing. No wonder they said Yugoslavia, even though it was a euphemistic anachronism – and we knew why!

This charming couple came to Mahabalipuram four years ago and fell in love with the area. He was obviously wealthy and she was obviously much younger. They flew from Belgrade to Madras via London, they told us. On their return they planned to spend four days in London. We got on so well that addresses were exchanged and mutual invitations to dinner were extended. She proffered her card which showed she was a radiologist by profession.

Then, up to our balcony for a pot of tea. We watched the boats in the distance as the sun went down. We were so sad to leave this glorious spot. *Désolés!*

Rusi arrived promptly at 7 p.m. and off we went to the vegetarian restaurant at Hotel Veelas. We were shown to a table in the courtyard surrounded by the bedrooms.

'Have you ever stayed here, Rusi?' Maggie asked, as newcomers with cases arrived and were quickly shown upstairs.

To our surprise he answered, 'I'm staying here now,' and

gave an impish, inscrutable grin. No more was said.

The food here was excellent – as good as last time. Puris, brinjal, vegetable curry, parotta and naan bread, were followed by ice cream and jelly – and all for £7. We agreed it was excellent value.

When we came back to our room, it was welcomingly cool and we prepared to spend our final night in the Ideal Resort at Mahabalipuram.

'It's been a great treat, Mac,' said Maggie. 'The only thing I didn't like was the crows.'

thursday, 8 february

Our travelling alarm clock woke us at 7 a.m. It was time to pack our cases. We put all that we needed for Puttaparthi in Maggie's case; mine was to be left in The Garden of Allah in Whitefield, Bangalore, and at 8.30 a.m. we went for our last swim. Heigh-ho! We so enjoyed our swimming. There had been no one else in the water every morning.

We went in for breakfast to find that the staff had already started clearing it away. We saw the Yugoslav couple again; they were uncertain about having a room at the hotel that night as it was being taken over by a group of Indian students. So there might be no room at the inn. We had a huge meal after which I settled the bill. It came to £140 for four days of bliss! We said goodbye to the manager and departed, sad but resigned. A new chapter beckoned.

We had another wonderful drive. There was always so much to see. We went through village after village, and then reached the amazing town of Kancheepuram – home of silk saris and temples. We stopped outside a temple to 'click' and gave one of the smiling children a green pen. The family looked delightedly on and waved animatedly as we departed. We were pursued through the streets of the town by silk agents on bikes, urging us to go to their factories and sample their wares. Maggie, with much reluctance, turned down their invitations, and on we went. Apparently, according to Rusi, Indian women come from all parts of the country to purchase their saris for their local weddings. He was uncertain as to the cost.

Through the town next, and on to Bangalore. We stopped for a cup of coffee in one of the Tamil Nadu hotels (a state-owned group whose hostelries we chose to avoid if at all possible – they are so dirty and uninviting.)

Maggie opened her sandwiches which were made and packed by the Ideal Resort chef in Mahabalipuram. They were good of their kind, but Maggie was 'cheesed off' with sandwiches.

There followed another eight hours of travelling on a very good road through varied and interesting scenery. Much of the terrain was very rocky and huge boulders littered the roadside. There were a great number of palm trees, and coconuts are available on wayside stalls. There were bullock carts in abundance, many painted blue to match the horns of the bullocks. Other horns were topped with gold to signify the affluence of the owner.

We had a very long wait at a railway crossing and Maggie took advantage of the delay to photograph a buffalo.

At 5 p.m. we stopped at Woody's for a snack. We had a delicious buttered dosa and tomato sandwiches, which we ordered from a very pushy waiter. Another poor loo to add to our growing list...

At 6 p.m. we arrived at Mr Patel's guest house opposite Baba's ashram in Bangalore. We had the use of a pretty green garden and a good basic room for £6 a night. Apparently the room cost double last week when Baba was here. Such is the appeal of Baba!

An hour later we were picked up by one of Rusi's drivers and conveyed to Rusi's house. Rusi, as host, took on our holiday tradition of drinks and nibbles, opening the red wine we had given him and Dinu as a gift. It was a very good wine – Chateau Bordeaux. We then went to a restaurant in Whitefield, where the food was both good and cheap, the bill amounting to £6 for four. Incredible. Throughout the meal, Dinu was very forthright, and spoke to the waiters as if they were her boys. Rusi, on the other hand, was very quiet and subdued.

Dinu told us that Ishver had contacted the Prince Café in Puttaparthi to tell of his arrival in the ashram. With any luck we'd see him, Baba willing! There's no such thing as coincidence!

We went to bed very tired and slept extremely well.

friday, 5 february

'Happy, happy birthday, dear Hannah!' was on our lips and our minds as we roused ourselves early. We saw Mr Patel and I paid him for the night's lodging. He said it would be all right to stay another night on our return from Puttaparthi, though he personally would be away in Gujarat visiting relatives who have survived the earthquake.

We were delighted when Ashok called to pick us up. Ashok is a senior driver of Rusi's; we hadn't been driven by him for three years and we had such vivid memories of shared experiences. Maggie was upset because she had failed to find a photograph which she took of him all that time ago – and she packed it carefully in London! Where was it? It would turn up, no doubt. But when? Too late, probably.

We had a lovely breakfast with Dinu: omelettes with onion and super toast and butter.

Now it was time to say goodbye to Rusi. He was unable to drive us to Puttaparthi because of other business commitments. Maggie was emotional. She bade him a tearful farewell, unable to contemplate further travels without Rusi. He had shared our experiences for nearly three weeks and we had not had a single altercation. He had guided us and advised us, and generally looked after us throughout our long and varied journey. I, too, was sad.

However, he said that he would come and pick us up at Puttaparthi and that his home would always be our home. He now dreamt of owning a guest house and wanted us to come whenever we needed it. I am sure it will happen.

Rusi's dreams have a way of becoming reality.

Before we left I paid him £150, making £600 in all, which was about £30 per day for petrol and personal care. I was well satisfied.

Our driver was Prabinja, another of Rusi's boys. He dropped me at Thomas Cook's, where I cashed a £50 traveller's cheque which will last, I hope, for the rest of the holiday.

We had another passenger in the car – Elrika – a wealthy, elderly German woman, who was a devotee of Baba and had a flat opposite Rusi's house in Whitefield.

Maggie, who readily admits to a certain prejudice against the nation which compelled her father to don an ARP helmet during the last war in Swansea, was not best pleased. I did most of the talking in the early stages.

Gradually, Maggie thawed out, as she put it later, and the conversation improved.

Maggie was particularly anxious to telephone Hannah, as it was her birthday. Prabinja obligingly stopped at two kiosks but we failed to get through. However, perseverance finally paid off, and the third time we were lucky. It was 7.30 a.m. in Brecon, and Hannah was about to go through the door to her office in the town. It was wonderful to hear her and chat to her on this, her special day.

Telephone call over, we resumed our journey. Five minutes later we were forced off the road as a lorry nearly crashed into us. *Oh Rusi, where are you?* It wasn't Prabinja's fault, I hasten to add, but Rusi is special. This kind of thing just wouldn't happen with him. He is always one jump ahead.

We stopped at a wayside café. It was dirty and uninviting; not on Rusi's list, I suspect. Maggie purchased four bananas after we had finished our coffees.

Maggie needed the loo but elected to go in the country. We got in the car and drove off. In suitable terrain, where there were plenty of bushes, Prabinja stopped. I always accompanied Maggie on these sorties to protect her from snakes. Fortunately, snakes are nocturnal creatures, and the likelihood of seeing one was remote.

When we returned it became apparent that Elrika was something of an expert on snakes. She told us that she was once in an ashram in Delhi and saw a cobra in a loo pan. She looked it straight in the eye and it withdrew whence it came, down the drain. Apparently if you stand still – motionless – they'll retreat. As if! I just hope and pray that I never have to put Elrika's theory to the test.

Elrika was now in her element and pointed out large mounds of brown earth which she identified as snake houses; and indeed you could see the holes they make leaving and entering the mound. Compared to molehills they were mountains. How strange we had never been instructed about 'snake houses' before. We must have passed hundreds during our time in India. I'd have to question Rusi about this. The snakes would be sleeping in there at that very moment! Maggie shivered at the thought.

The scenery was becoming increasingly beautiful and the villages more and more affluent as we approached Puttaparthi. The earth was a rich red and brown, and the roadsides were strewn with boulders topped by palm trees.

Elrika experienced difficulty in walking as she has had both legs broken in an unfortunate experience with Baba's elephant. She was approaching the elephant when it reared up! Affrighted, Elrika staggered back, fell awkwardly and shattered both legs.

After lengthy surgery she was able to walk, but it affected her mobility considerably. The incident did not, however, affect her faith in Baba or his elephant.

We dropped her off at Prince's Café and then proceeded to the Sri Renaissance Hotel. We discovered that we had not been booked in, but not to worry, there were plenty of rooms available. The room cost £9, which was good value.

I handed over our passports to the young man at the desk and incurred my wife's wrath when I told her this in the bedroom. I had broken one of Rusi's prime rules and was despatched forthwith to recover the irreplaceable documents. I was sure the boy was trustworthy but, as Maggie insisted, that was not the point. I think he's a little starstruck as he was hugely impressed when he learned my profession. In India, Bollywood stars are revered like Gods, hence this reaction, as I am an actor.

After a cup of tea (room service) we unpacked and then went to Prince's Café. The time was 4 p.m. Zarrine, Rusi's sister, was there in her capacity as manageress, and she welcomed us with her usual warmth. We had bottled water, cappuccino, buttered dosas and spaghetti. I also had pineapple and cheese toast. Wonderful – and all for 173 rupees!

Zarrine insisted on taking time off work to accompany Maggie to the silk merchant. In actual fact, it was Maggie who remembered which one we used last time, as Zarrine mistakenly suggested another one.

The staff of the shop were just as we remembered them and just as obliging. After protracted negotiations, which we all enjoyed, Maggie elected to have a Punjabi suit in grey, a grey silk shirt and a black trouser suit. The total cost of labour and materials was agreed at £47, after a great deal of good-natured bargaining and banter. Maggie achieved a discount of £10.

Zarrine contributed to the discussion on colours but left Maggie to arrange the price.

Afterwards, Zarrine took us to Bhajans: there we separated. Bhajans is a prayer session attended by Sai Baba, interspersed with music and song. Zarrine and Maggie joined the women and I went with the men. I found this segregation unsettling and unnecessary. I was frisked by the security men and then allowed into the temple where, cross-legged, we awaited Baba's impending arrival. All around, the devotees were excited and chanting animatedly. There were people of all ages, races and creeds, all eagerly awaiting the entrance of Swami. At the appointed hour the music stopped, the lights increased and a bell tolled with rapid momentum. At that precise moment, Baba, in an orange robe, glides into the full view of the expectant assembly. His entry is most impressive. He walks towards the women, smiling. He looks the same as he did three years ago, but thinner perhaps. As he moves there is a shaft of light upon him.

I looked around in the vain hope of seeing Ishver in the gathered thousands. It was his birthday as well as Hannah's. Perhaps he would come to Prince's Café today or tomorrow. It would be impossible to see him here, or would it? Perhaps Baba could arrange a meeting.

After Bhajans, we went back to Prince's Café where we met a girl from Llanelli. She was very young and on her own – obviously another female devotee besotted by Baba.

'I thought I knew all the devotees from Wales,' she said.

Just before dark we walked about the ashram. In the midst of the activity there was an air of tranquillity. There was a huge sound of birds from the trees in the centre of the ashram. Then we saw egrets flying over Baba's house.

Tired and exhausted, we returned to the hotel by 7 p.m. Once back in the bedroom, Maggie was in pensive mood. She confided that on entering Puttaparthi she saw, through the car window, a tree growing on the top of a pile of boulders and for some reason she was deeply moved by the experience. She suddenly felt at peace. She felt it was miraculous to be back once more in Puttaparthi.

At 8 p.m. we went downstairs to the hotel restaurant, which appeared much improved. We ordered tomato soup from a charming waiter, followed by a puri for Maggie and a baked bean toasted sandwich for me. I had a lassi and Maggie had a ginger tea.

As we ate, a smartly dressed manager, tall with glasses, cream trousers and a green shirt, approached our table and stared, then he said, 'Are you from the UK?'

'Yes.'

'You have been here before?'

'Yes, twice.'

Then, looking hard at Maggie, he said, 'Are you better now?'

'Yes, thank you.'

'You are OK.'

There is no way he could have been informed of Maggie's recent illness. It was astonishing. I was deeply moved and felt that it was the work of Baba. I said this to Maggie. What other explanation was there? Rusi didn't know the staff at this hotel, and his boy, whom we don't know, booked the room.

Maggie was amazed and didn't know what to say!

We hadn't spoken to Myf for over a week, which was hard on Maggie, who usually speaks to her every day. She suggested we try her now at work before she left for the weekend. So we crossed the wasteland near the hotel to reach the nearest kiosk. The street dogs were howling like banshees. The boy in the kiosk tried to connect us but every time her number was engaged.

We concluded that his phone must be faulty, and tried our luck in another booth run by a pretty girl.

Straight through this time. We just caught Myf before she left for Ireland. She and John were flying there at 7.30 p.m. They were going to Cathy's wedding. Cathy is a mutual friend from university days at Bangor. We reassured each other that all was well. 'If it wasn't, she wouldn't tell us,' murmured Maggie. Myf kept asking if she and John could come with us next time. 'Of course, of course,' we chorused. 'You'll love it, and so would Rusi.' Which is true!

We replaced the receiver, paid the girl and left. Four swarthy men sitting outside said '*Sai Ram*' to us. People are so friendly around here. We felt safe.

The love generated by Baba has a direct influence on all these people's lives, and with that love comes a sense of peace and security.

'Do not fear when I am here.'

Maggie told me how much she valued Zarrine's friendship and what a lovely person she is. I agreed, and we looked forward to having dinner with her at our hotel tomorrow. She certainly accepted the invitation with alacrity, so we presumed our feelings were mutual.

saturday, 10 february

Neither of us slept well. We were too churned up with the Baba experience. There is always something special about Swami's ashram. There is always the anticipation of the unexpected. You feel Baba makes things happen. The street dogs howled disturbingly.

We woke at 8 a.m. and went down to breakfast. Delicious toast and marmalade and large glasses of coffee. Maggie had fresh pineapple juice too, which she loves.

At 9 a.m. we rushed to Bhajans and went our separate ways. Maggie was frisked and told to wear a petticoat in future by a slip of a girl. 'Bloody cheek!' muttered Maggie.

Once again Maggie was lucky. Baba moved or rather glided towards the ladies' section after he had made his exit towards his house. The devotees followed at a respectful distance and bent to touch the lotus flower on which his feet had trod.

Maggie was very moved to follow in the master's footsteps.

I, meanwhile, encountered Ishver in a weird and wonderful way.

Rejecting the idea of seeing Ishver among so many thousands, I decided not to linger longer inside the temple but turn towards the exit in order to rejoin Maggie under the bougainvillea tree. After having gone a few steps, I suddenly felt I must return and have one last look at the interior of the temple. As I turned, directly in front of me I saw Ishver. I couldn't believe it! It was a miracle. Surely it must have been preordained, to see Ishver among so many thousands. It was a most moving experience. He instinctively took my hand and we walked like children towards Ganesh. It was a moment of innocent celebration.

Reunited with Maggie, Ishver told us that since his arrival in Puttaparthi he had been appointed to a senior position within the UK Sai Baba Organisation – a prestigious honour – and we congratulated him warmly. However, he was still worried about Baba as he has not been granted an interview. 'Will it happen tomorrow?' he wondered.

Meanwhile, he had to meet an important member of Baba's hierarchy at 10 a.m. and would join us afterwards in Prince's Café about 10.30 a.m.

In the event, we missed him, as he was punctual and we were not. He had to leave straight away as he was expecting an important phone call from Italy.

Before we left the café, Maggie and I had a cheese sandwich and then made our way to our favourite garden in the ashram. We particularly remembered the gold statue of Jesus depicting him as the shepherd with a lamb. Maggie sat and finished her postcards while I sat and read, pausing periodically for meditation.

Lunch hour approached, so we returned to Princes Café for lunch where we sampled an awful tomato omelette and good French fries. Fortunately, Zarrine wasn't there so we could leave the omelettes.

Back to our Garden of Rest, with its statues representative of all the religions. We sat on a very hard seat and dozed in the sunshine. A young devotee sat near us in a supervisory capacity to see that there was no – as Maggie puts it – 'hanky panky'.

At 3 p.m. the peace of the garden was shattered by the music of the Darshan, so we moved on to the ashram post office, with which we were very impressed. It was highly efficient and obviously accustomed to handling international mail. The Darshan is an afternoon session at which Baba also appears.

A quick visit to the silk merchant confirmed that Maggie's clothes would be ready for collection at 6 p.m. after Bhajan.

There was just time for toast and coffee at the hotel before we returned post haste to the ashram for Bhajans. I was misguidedly under the impression that we had come to India for a rest!

Taking up her place in the temple, Maggie had another brush with Baba's handmaidens. Apparently, her petticoat was too short this time. Maggie had to promise to comply with the regulations next time. As she said later to me, 'It is extraordinary that I cover my shoulders with a scarf while most of the saris on show display all the midriff, which is, after all, undeniably, a much more erogenous zone. Ah, well!'

The women, it would appear, are ghastly, pushing and shoving to achieve a better vantage point from which to view Swami sitting on his throne. Suddenly there is silence and he moves inside while the chanting begins.

After another impressive ceremony Maggie, Ishver and I made our separate ways to the bougainvillea tree near the statue of Ganesh. Ishver wanted us all to stroll around the ashram, but Maggie had to collect her silken garments. So we excused ourselves and went to the silk merchant. We had invited Ishver to dine with us in the evening but he did not like leaving the precincts of the ashram. Once there, he rarely set foot outside. It interfered with his spiritual concentration and contentment – a point of view with which we fully sympathise as, outside the gates of the ashram, we felt, as Wordsworth says:

> The world is too much with us; late and soon
> Getting and spending...*

---

* From: Wordsworth, William 'The World is Too Much With Us'

We returned to Room 19 in the hotel clutching Maggie's purchases. She tried them on in nervous anticipation. They are wonderful. The grey material of the shirt was so unusual. Maggie was a little worried about a flaw in the material of the Punjabi tunic, but we agreed that on inspection it was scarcely noticeable. So we decided that it was OK, and we were well pleased with those recent additions to her wardrobe.

Zarrine and Rusi arrived for supper and we had a very jolly evening. During the course of the supper, Rusi was approached by an anxious Australian lady who needed his help and advice. Apparently, she was terminally ill and relied very heavily on Rusi. He agreed to speak with her later and we proceeded with our supper. Delicious tomato soup, buttered naan bread, Manchurian cauliflower, cashew nut curry, which was unbelievably tasty, white rice and ice cream. £10 for three courses for four people! Wow!

We escorted our friends to the door. They had been wonderful guests, so jolly and appreciative. The cicadas were very noisy tonight. Zarrine calls them 'bee-bees'.

What a remarkable day! To see Ishver in the ashram and to be there all day. It had been exceptionally hectic but memorable.

sunday, 11 february

The penultimate day of our holiday.

We woke about 7 a.m. after a 'brill' night's sleep. We didn't hear a sound. No street dogs; nothing. We packed up quickly and I washed my hair. Down to breakfast. Lovely toast and marmalade, a big bowl of cornflakes with cold milk, and large glasses of coffee. I settled the bill, paying £18 for two nights, which we both agreed was money well spent. The owner was in attendance and was charming. Maggie bought two more elephants from the hotel shop for ninety rupees each. We'd need a bigger table in England to accommodate our growing collection...

Rusi arrived. Apparently, the Australian lady who came to see him at supper last night – the one who was terminally ill – had hysterics in the night and sent for him. A doctor was called to inject her, and the long and short of it was that Rusi had agreed to drive her to Madras to put her on a plane, as she hadn't long to live. Baba drove past Rusi's office this morning and waved to him.

Rusi was now convinced that he was meant to drive the Australian lady, and had sent for Prabinja to come to Puttaparthi and drive us back to Bangalore.

Off to Bhajan where we thought of Myf and her painful neck, and Tony Clubb and Sue's brother, Robin, who had recently contracted cancer. We said goodbye to Swami and asked that we might return.

Afterwards, we were joined by Ishver at the bougainvillea tree and we took our leave of him. I knew he would miss us.

What a lovely man he is; kind, gentle and sensitive, with a twinkling sense of humour.

More farewells followed. At the Prince's Café we said goodbye to Zarrine, after a cursory call at the silk merchant's. Everyone seemed sad to see us go. After a quick lime soda, gripping a packet of cheese sandwiches made by Zarrine, we walked to Rusi's office at the other end of town.

There we found an American lady who was to accompany us on the journey. Her name was Tara, and she talked non-stop all the way to Bangalore. Apparently, she was an ardent devotee of Swami, like her daughter but not her sons, aged forty-one and thirty-nine respectively. She followed Baba wherever he went, but was based at the moment in a studio in Puttaparthi which she had bought. She became a devotee ten years ago after meeting Swami in a group. She told us the story of Rama, an old lady living beneath a building, who was persuaded by an enthusiastic group of devotees to enter a Mother Theresa home. She was unable to enter an ashram home as she couldn't look after herself. The Mother Superior told Rama how wonderful the home would be. 'You will have lovely sisters to look after you and congenial companions who will sit with you in a beautiful garden all day listening to music. Have you any questions, Rama?'

The old lady thought for a moment and then she said, 'Will I eat lamb as I used to do when I lived in Nepal?'

'Yes,' replied the Mother Superior, 'every Monday.'

So the deal was clinched and Rama entered the home and as far as Tara knew has lived there happily ever after; though she'd never been back to see, which I think said something about Tara and her zeal for helping others.

Maggie and I were worn out when our car stopped outside Mr Patel's.

At 3.30 p.m. Ashok arrived to take us to Bangalore. We drove for forty-five minutes through very heavy traffic. We parked where we used to three years ago, after several abortive attempts. What a busy city this is! There were two objectives for our shopping expedition: first, to replace my hand luggage bag, which was in a very fragile condition and had been for most of the holiday; and second, to buy the rest of the presents before we left India. Ashok took us to a bag shop where we purchased an excellent holdall for only £3.50. Then, in a nearby alleyway, Maggie employed her bargaining skills to obtain three leather belts at very reduced prices. She had become so good at it!

Ashok, who was proving an excellent guide, showed us MG Road, which is Mahatma Ghandi Road to the initiated. It is an extremely busy thoroughfare – the Oxford Street of Bangalore. We were so engrossed in the silk shops that our initial tiredness evaporated.

We were feeling in need of refreshment, so Ashok took us to a good restaurant where we had pineapple juice, buttered dosas, tea and salad sandwiches. Ashok had apple juice. The restaurant looked unpromising from the outside but it proved to be authentically Indian, full of shoppers taking a Saturday break.

We arrived back in Mr Patel's at 6.15 p.m. and sent a message to Dinu via Ashok. We would like to dine at 7.30 p.m. if she would care to join us. At 7.20 p.m., with typical Dinu efficiency, she arrived and whisked us off to the same restaurant, and we sat in the same corner as before. Maggie was a little cross as there were heaps of tables in the garden but she showed remarkable restraint and said nothing. The light was very limited and we had to peer at the menu before making our considered selection. In the event, we had a very pleasant meal. Dinu was in very good form and made us laugh a lot with stories of Elrika and other devotees. On a more serious note, she described the Parsee funeral – customs which we find a little macabre. Apparently, in accordance with Parsee rites, the body of

Dinu's mother was taken to the Fire Temple, where it was placed on a marble slab in a well, and the vultures came and quickly devoured her flesh. Prayers are said for four days and on the fourth day God decides the fate of the soul. It goes to one out of seven possible realms. We found this insight into Indian funeral customs extremely interesting, as we ate our crispy noodles with egg fried rice, Manchurian vegetables and chicken chop suey, and drank our Kingfisher beers.

Rusi phoned on his mobile at 8.30 p.m. from Madras. He told Dinu that the Australian lady was on the plane. He'd sleep in the car for two hours and then drive home through the night.

Dinu was on a high and told us that we could always find out the time in England by looking at our watches upside down.

We discuss the guru, Sri Maharshi, whom Tara told us about on the car journey earlier today. He has a lovely face and wears only a white diaper. The ashram is at Tiruvannamalai, near to Pondicherry. It is very beautiful, located near a mountain. Maggie was impressed that his mother lived nearby and worshipped at the Ashram.

We also discussed the bossy handmaidens at Baba's ashram – the 'Serva Dal' as they are called. We learnt that they are volunteers who officiate for three months at a time. They are graduates of Baba's College and come to Whitefields with him.

In a very happy frame of mind, we returned to our cottage. On the way in we saw a person sleeping in a rug on the stone floor outside the office. He was completely enveloped but we concluded that he must be the servant.

monday, 12 february

Still in bed at 9 a.m. when there was a knock on the door.

'I've come to get you to breakfast.'

It was Dinu. Maggie realised that Rusi had returned from Madras and would naturally worry about Maggie's need for an early breakfast. Hence the visit.

Over we went to The Garden of Allah, where we were greeted by Rusi, tired but cheerful after his lengthy journey. His mission had been successfully carried out and the Australian lady was now on her way to Australia.

We had a very tasty breakfast of omelettes, toast and coffee, and then went back to the cottage with all our possessions, including the items stored with Rusi.

The first task was to pack for the flight home, scheduled for midnight that night. We sorted out all our possessions and then allocated them to the two cases and hand luggage containers. Fortunately, everything fitted in.

Then we settled down to read our books in this very pretty garden, realising that this was probably our last chance of sunbathing for a very long time. Weather reports from England had been atrocious.

Suddenly, at 1 p.m., Dinu arrived. 'Change of plan,' she said with characteristic abruptness. She had to meet someone at the airport, and Rusi was asleep. However, we were not to be denied lunch. It was a case of 'meals on wheels': a lovely curry in containers, as well as a carrot and tomato salad. We sat at our table and ate it all, every scrap, and laughed. Rusi and Dinu thrive on crises and they stagger from one to another. But with all those servants they can cope with anything.

Maggie and I slept until 3.15 p.m. It was so peaceful in our cottage and garden. Then we walked across the road to phone Hannah. It would be 9.45 a.m. in England and she was having a birthday weekend in 'Y Freni'. It was simply marvellous to hear her voice. She was thrilled. She loved the tartan pyjamas we gave her for her birthday. Next weekend she would come home again to go with us to the National Theatre to see *The Cherry Orchard*. Talking with her, Maggie and I realised that we were now ready to return home. We missed 'Y Freni' and home comforts; in particular we longed for a bath! There's no place like home... though this had been one of the best holidays ever.

We sat in the sun surrounded by wonderful flowers and read. Mr Patel, we concluded, was a very shrewd man. He has between fifty and sixty apartments.

About 6.30 p.m. we began to worry as there has been no word from Rusi. I crossed the road to telephone him for two rupees. He reassured me that he would be with us in half an hour. They were making sandwiches for Maggie as he spoke.

Dinu and Rusi were as good as their word and arrived at the appointed hour. In three-quarters of an hour, we arrived at Bangalore Airport. It was very crowded. Our friends offered to buy us supper but we refused. We wanted to go now. Maggie gave Rusi her Hermesetas sweeteners as we parted, since he had shared them with her throughout the trip. They handed over a big box of sandwiches.

As we embraced and parted, Dinu told us, 'You are not friends anymore, you are family.' That said it all.

CPSIA information can be obtained at www.ICGtesting.com
Printed in the USA
BVOW08s1955121215

430096BV00001B/9/P